The Bat Tattoo

The Bat Tattoo

Russell Hoban

BLOOMSBURY

Grateful acknowledgement is
made to Hornall Brothers Music Limited for permission to
quote from 'Is That All There Is' by Leiber/Stoller.

First published 2002
This paperback edition published 2003

Bloomsbury Publishing Plc, 38 Soho Square,
London W1D 3HB

A CIP catalogue record for this
book is available from the British Library

ISBN 07475 6163 X

10 9 8 7 6 5 4 3 2 1

All papers used by Bloomsbury Publishing are
natural, recyclable products made from wood
grown in sustainable, well-managed forests.
The manufacturing processes conform to the
environmental regulations of the country of origin.

Typeset by Palimpsest Book Production Limited,
Polmont, Stirlingshire

Printed by Clays Ltd, St Ives plc

To Gundel

Nur die Fülle führt zur Klarheit,
Und im Abgrund wohnt die Wahrheit.
Schiller

ACKNOWLEDGEMENTS

For help in my researches, given most graciously, I am
indebted to: Justine Lewis and Ming Wilson of the
Far Eastern Department of the Victoria & Albert Museum;
Lorraine Bewick, Anthony Green, and Henry Grey of
Alec Tiranti Ltd; Stuart Duncan of Moss & Co; Mick Corbett
and Gary Maclaren of the Fulham Tattoo Centre; Father John
Hunter of the Parish Church of St John, Walham Green;
Jane Pountney; Cathy Price of the Cranbrook Archive;
Stanley Levy; Robert Ellis; and my son Ben. Dominic Power
read many drafts and gave me useful comments. My wife
Gundula assisted in innumerable ways in London and Autun.

Whichever way you turn,
your arse stays always behind.

German folk-saying

1

ROSWELL CLARK

I thought a tattoo might be a good move. I'd reached the age of forty-seven without one but maybe the time had come. In one of my books there's a photograph of a nineteenth-century Chinese chair cover with two really happy-looking bats on it and I imagined one of those bats on my shoulder bringing me luck. The chair cover was at the Victoria & Albert Museum so I went there to check it out.

It was one of those global-warming March days: people opening coats and jackets or carrying them. Tourists with maps and guides going up and down the steps while a woman sat there looking up at the grey sky with tears running down her face. There are benches to the right of the entrance but she was on those concrete steps which have very short risers; sitting on them brings your knees up too high – OK for a crying teenager but this was a woman in her mid-forties who didn't strike me as a public crier. A big woman; even sat down she looked tall and broad with a strong weatherbeaten face, ruddy complexion, wide mouth, heroic nose. Almost I smelled salt air, saw her among barrels and cordage with other women at a long table filleting herring. Or pacing the shore, her shawl whipping in the wind, her eye to the sea.

When she saw me watching her she put her hand over her eyes. She had mousy hair, pulled back and held with a thick rubber band so that it hung down her back a little way. Black woollen cap, grey jumper, blue anorak, dark-grey long skirt, thick-soled boots with a lot of mileage on them. Heavy-looking shoulder bag beside her.

'Are you all right?' I asked her.

'I'm fine.' Looked at me a little angrily, I thought. Steely blue eyes. Talked posh, a low fruity voice like what was her name? Charlotte Green. Used to do late news or the shipping forecast on the World Service, maybe both. I have her on tape; she said 'Dogger Bank' in a way that made me want to drop everything and ship out on a North Sea trawler.

'You don't look fine,' I said.

'What I mean is, I don't need help.'

I was about to say that everybody needs help but I decided not to. 'OK, I'll leave you to it then.'

Before going in I turned to look at the traffic on the Cromwell Road. The cars, buses, and lorries all had places to go but I wondered how much difference it would make if they all went somewhere else. I usually have a song going in my head; this time it was 'Is That All There Is?' as sung by Peggy Lee.

In my rucksack was the book with a photograph of the chair cover; it was blue silk with a golden Chinese unicorn on it, and above the unicorn the two bats, one on either side; nothing spooky, they were dancing in that blue-silk sky like paper kites, their fancy wings all curvy and fringy. Getting one of those bats tattooed on my shoulder would be a big step for me – I wanted a closer look and I'd brought a camera with me hoping to get a little more detail than the picture in the book.

I showed the book to a woman at the information desk; she phoned a colleague but couldn't locate the chair cover so she gave me a map and directed me to the Chinese gallery. By then the song in my head had changed to 'From This Moment On' as sung by Dad and I couldn't help smiling at that.

I have a Friends card; I like the way they nod me through when I show it: I'm not a stranger. I always feel good in museums. I like the high ceilings and the acoustics, the footsteps and the voices, the silence over and under the footsteps and voices and the individual silences of each thing, all of them different, all of them holding a long-departed Now.

Looking for a particular thing in a museum is like looking for a word in the dictionary – you keep being led astray. Bodhisattvas, Buddhist banners, bronze and jade and robes with dragons. Little earthenware ladies out of tombs: their robes were glazed, their faces not, their mouths were closed. Horses, T'ang Dynasty – their saddles were empty, waiting to take the dead to paradise. Just looking at those horses you could hear the clip-clop of their hooves in the silence.

There was a little bronze tomb guardian, something between a dog and a nightmare, who looked as if he could lick his weight in demons or anything else that came his way. Although I wasn't dead I felt safer with him around. A place like that Chinese gallery is bound to be haunted by ghosts, demons, who knows what. For that matter, every place I know is haunted by ghosts, demons, and absent friends. There were all kinds of things in that gallery but no chair cover and no bats.

After a while I found myself in front of a large display case with a wonderful ivory boat model in it. It was about two feet long and it was a kind of floating double-decker pleasure garden with banners and lanterns on poles and a mast with what might be a torch basket near the top. The various roofs, doors, windows and sidings were elaborately carved and filigreed. On the upper deck was a dining pavilion; were those flowers on the table, bottles of wine? The boat was being poled along by four crewmen in elegant robes and red caps whose poles reached only to the little square of glass the model rested on. A fifth man was in the bows with what might have been a sounding pole. A card lying on the surface of the square glass river said:

MODEL OF A BOAT
Carved and painted ivory, with
clockwork motor,
About 1800.
This model was brought to England
in 1803 by Richard Hall
(1764–1834), who had been head of the
English factory at Canton.

Looking at that boat I wanted to be aboard it, cruising down a river of dreams while the polesmen stood motionless, the clockwork slowly unwound, and on either side passed the banks of a country never seen before. I cruised for a minute or two on the river of dreams but it flowed past scenes of my Michigan childhood, the white clapboard house in Ferndale, the Orpheus fountain at Cranbrook with the bronze figures stretching their arms towards music they couldn't hear; it flowed past years of my London life, evening lights and happiness on Hungerford Bridge, Sunday walks along the river, and the crunching impact of metal on metal on a rainy night near King's Cross. It flowed past tourists sitting on benches in the hall that went through China and Korea, and when I saw a guard I stepped ashore and asked for directions to the nearest bat. He didn't know, he said, but try Level D, Chinese ceramics.

Leaving Level A China I took a shortcut through the sculpture gallery and stopped to say hello to Handel. He was very casual in dressing-gown, nightcap, and slippers (one on and one off), stroking his lyre while a putto leant against his leg and took notes. The maestro was fully clothed under the dressing-gown but the putto of course was starkers. An elderly couple paused in front of the pair.

'Puttophile?' said the man.

'It was a different time,' said the wife. 'There were always putti knocking about in artists' studios then.'

With a little guidance from the cloakroom attendant I took the stairs to Lower A, walked east for ten minutes or so past a great many things in bronze, wood, and china, found the lift, and went up to Level D. No bats right off but I had to stop and admire a 'Model of a Daoist temple and adjacent landscape. Ivory and wood, with mother-of-pearl, semi-precious stones and metals. Chinese, about 1800.' This was a temple on its own little mountain, with various outbuildings, a tower and a willow-pattern bridge with what looked like one of the chaps from the ivory boat on it, apparently part of a procession to the temple. Might there have been a race of tiny Cantonese working night and day to build the boat and the temple for the export trade? And when the job was done some hand, of a Chinese Vincent Price perhaps, touched them into ivory stillness and here they were. The card went on to say that the model 'was acquired by the Museum of the Honourable East India Co. in 1810. It was believed to have been intended as a present for Josephine Buonaparte'. I wondered why she never got it.

I turned left, went round a corner, and there was a display case with various crockery on shelves. The woman who'd been crying on the steps was planted in front of it. Looking past her shoulder I saw a small bowl and a larger one, both with bats on them. The small bowl was pale green, the larger one white; the bats on both were red. I moved closer to see better and caught a faint scent of honeysuckle. Evidently I moved closer than I ought to have done because she turned and gave me a hard smile and said, 'If you were a bit taller you'd be breathing down my neck.'

'Sorry, I'll go away and come back later. Do you think you'll be finished here in fifteen minutes or so?'

She looked me up and down and I had a feeling that she didn't like Americans. She was about six feet tall which made it more so. 'I'm finished now,' she said. 'You've seen to that.' She planted her foot on my chest, pulled out her spear, climbed into her chariot, and drove off, leaving me feeling surprisingly tired from so brief an encounter but free to give my full attention to the bats.

The card for the larger bowl described it as a 'Lobed bowl, painted with bats, a symbol of happiness. Mark and Reign period of Yongzheng, 1722–1735. Julia C. Gulland gift.' As I stood directly in front of it two of the lobes were visible with a pair of bats on each. In each pair one bat was pointing up and the other down. Their flight seemed full of unquenchable high spirits. They made the chair-cover bats look repressed, inhibited. The bottom one on the right, the upward-flying bat, was the one that I liked best: it was a Let's-do-it! bat. Do what? No idea, but I could already feel it on my shoulder bringing me luck. Most of the time people wouldn't know it was there but I would and it would make a big difference.

Batting a thousand and feeling good I took out my little

Olympus mju-II which was loaded with Fuji 1600. The skylights ran the full length of the gallery and the daylight was more than adequate but just to be sure I shot the bowl with flash and without, from about a foot and a half and from further away. 'Well done,' I said, and put my camera back in the rucksack.

I had the bat I wanted but I felt, I don't know, that I could have been a bit more of a gentleman in my second encounter with Boadicea. More English. Now that my bat was safely aboard I found myself wondering what her connection with it was. There were other non-bat bowls in that display case and there were other bats visible on the two bowls with bats but she'd been talking to my particular bat – it's the kind of thing one instinctively knows. What did it mean to her?

I tried to guess what kind of life she had. Divorced, I thought, not widowed. Living on alimony? Maybe she had some kind of business. No nail polish. Did she do something with her hands? Antiques or something arts-and-craftsy? Maybe widowed, come to think of it – she could have worn the guy out. But the bat? A nocturnal animal. Was she a night person? Was the night a special time for her the way it is for me? 'A symbol of happiness'. Was she looking for happiness? Not me. I was only looking for my self.

2

SARAH VARLEY

God, am I going to become an embarrassment to myself?
Crying on the steps of the V & A! Not even on a bench but
right there on the steps where people had to walk around me.
A cry for help? From whom, from what? What am I going
to do next, wander the streets in a nightdress?

The morning started off all right. I had a whole clear
day ahead of me, nothing coming up except Chelsea on
Saturday. Poached egg on toast, grapefruit juice, tea with
lemon and *The Times*. I never bother with the top of the
front page – it's always some politician lying or cheat-
ing or caught with his trousers down. But there on the
bottom:

WE'VE GOT ONLY 500M YEARS
LEFT TO LIVE

The end of the world really is in sight. Scientists studying
the fate of the Earth have warned that the expansion of
the Sun will turn it into a desert in 500m years, much
sooner than previously thought, *write Polly Ghazi and
Jonathan Leake*.

The story went on to explain how this prediction had been arrived at; it seemed that previous calculations had given the Earth five billion years but suddenly, like Christmas, it was almost upon us. I'll be long gone, I told myself, but it didn't help. I reached inside my robe and touched my bat but that didn't help either.

I suppose in five hundred million years Earth will long since have been deserted and there will be Earthlings living under domes on Mars and elsewhere but it won't be the same, it won't be Earth where when I was young you could sleep under the stars and wake up to see the mist rising from a lake you could swim in without vomiting. Earth where there used to be the Taj Mahal and the Himalayas, Bengal tigers and Peter Rabbit, Claude and Chardin and Haydn and *The Goon Show*. And eighteenth-century Chinese bowls with red bats, 'symbol of happiness'. That's when I started crying and I needed to go and look at my bat.

I splashed cold water on my face before I left and I was all right from my house down the New Kings Road to Parsons Green Lane and the tube station, still all right up the stairs and on to the platform. The sky was grey, it looked as if it no longer believed in itself.

A young woman stood near me on the platform: dark hair, short bob, dressed for business in a black suit, knee-length skirt, transparent black tights, black court shoes, lilac silk T-shirt, large black leather shoulder bag. Very attractive, with a sombre expression. She was reading the Penguin edition of *The Bridge of San Luis Rey* when her mobile rang and she reached into the bag for it.

'Hi,' she said. I liked her voice. Pause. 'Go ahead, I can talk.' Pause. 'We've been over this before, and you knew very well what you were getting into.' Pause. 'I know.' Pause. 'I know, Hilary, but this was not a for ever thing. You'd have liked there to be more but that's all there was, so now you've got to move on to the next thing.' Pause. 'No, it isn't easy for me to say, nothing's easy for me. Here comes my train, I'll talk to you later. Bye for now.' She replaced the phone; there was no train in sight, and she returned to *The Bridge of San Luis Rey*.

When the train came we both got into the same carriage. She continued to read her book and I watched her and thought about her all the way to South Kensington. Was she breaking up with Hilary or only offering friendly advice? Was Hilary a man or a woman? I had the feeling that Hilary was a woman, and the woman I was watching was breaking up with her. Hilary, it seemed, had expected more. Poor Hilary. A cool customer, this one in the train, but she didn't look very happy.

I never use the subway to the museums at South Ken; I don't like the footsteps and the echoes and I always want to see the sky during that little walk to Cromwell Road. As always, it was solid with traffic, blatant with purpose, filling the day with emptiness. What's happening to me? I thought – I didn't use to feel this way.

The front of the V & A was partly covered with hoarding and there were men in hard hats doing I don't know what. A white van with a ladder on top pulled up in front of the entrance steps and a hard-hat man got out, turned towards the workmen at the hoarding, and spoke into his mobile. For all I knew he was saying, 'OK, let's do it,' and in a moment they'd blow up the museum with everything in it, all those fragile beauties and all the ghosts that lived there. Well, I thought, my mind is doing this, it's nothing to do with me. But I was crying so I sat down on the steps.

There was this man, then, looking down at me and asking if I was all right. American. I don't always have the proper responses to well-meaning people – all kinds of things get in the way sometimes. There was nothing objectionable about him. He was wearing jeans, a green anorak and a broad-brimmed green canvas hat, Timberlake boots, and had a rucksack slung from one shoulder. He was about my age, perhaps a year or two older, with nothing at all memorable about him; I guessed he often had trouble catching the waiter's eye. I couldn't tell if he was a tourist or not. He spoke quietly and his accent wasn't as American as some I've heard. Maybe it was the state I was in, but he seemed a failed person to me. Failed at what? I don't know – there was just that air about him and it put me off. He looked as if he expected to be rebuffed and I suppose I was brusque with him because of that. He was persistent, though, and after I said I was fine he said I didn't look fine, so I told him I didn't need help and he finally moved on.

I went in, checked my things, took the lift to Level D, and turned the corner into the long daylit gallery eager for my fix. The cool grey light refreshed my spirit immediately; it was what these beautiful things lived in, the air they breathed, a medium of non-forgetting. There was no one else in the gallery.

I'm sure that other people have their little rituals; I can't be the only one. I took up my station facing the lobed bowl with the four red bats that were visible from where I stood. Mine is the lower one on the right, the upward-flying bat. With my right hand I reached into my jumper and touched the identical bat tattooed on my left shoulder. Ordinarily I do the whole thing in silence but this time I said very quietly, 'Yongzheng, this is Sarah Varley requesting permission to feel better.'

Just then I heard footsteps so I took my hand out of my jumper and tried to look like everyone else. Out of the corner of my eye I saw that it was the man who'd spoken to me on the steps. This time he just stood behind me trying to see around me until I turned and was rather unkind to him. His only response was to ask me if I'd be finished in fifteen minutes or so. Americans! There was nothing for me to do but walk away although I was sure that he had designs on my bat. I hadn't had my full fix and I was frustrated and deeply resentful at the intrusion.

I went round the corner towards the lift but then on impulse I moved back to where I could see him. He had his camera out and was taking pictures of the bowl with *my* bat. The day had started badly and now I seemed to be in danger of losing it altogether. Taking what was left of it back home was like carrying water in my hands.

What was my bat to that man? What did he want with it, why did he need it? Why couldn't he find something else to get interested in? That sort of thing happens to me too often at auctions: when I want something it attracts other dealers who jump in and even if it's a lot they don't fancy they'll bid it up out of sheer perversity and then drop out so I'm stuck with paying more than I'd planned to.

Between Earls Court and West Brompton the train stopped as if reality had run out of film and for a while there was silence except for a City type who said into his mobile, 'I'm stuck here between Earls Court and West Brompton.' When the train started he made another call and said, 'Now we're moving again.'

Think about something else, I said to myself. I thought about what I'd pack for Chelsea, reviewing costume jewellery, handbags, dresses, china, and various oddments. Should I loosen up and take the minaudière? I wondered. The hammer price at Christie's last year was two-forty and I'd been saving it as an investment but I needed to create some excitement at my stall so it mightn't be a bad idea to bring it out into the world. While imagining how it would look on the stall I found myself at home without having noticed how I got there. '*Collectors' Lot*, I'm home,' I said, and switched on Channel 4 in time to catch a man whose obsession was the history of dentures. 'Amazing,' said Debbie Thrower, flashing her own original dentition as he showed her a pair of Chinese choppers exquisitely carved in ivory. That reminded me that I had an appointment coming up in a fortnight with Mr Sharif for two implants in my lower jaw, so I switched off the denture man and went down to the kitchen to sort through my treasures.

'Yes!' I said, as my own space settled cosily around me. I took off my boots, got a started bottle of New Zealand Sauvignon blanc out of the fridge and poured myself a glass. 'There!' I said. 'That's better, isn't it? At least if he gets my bat tattooed on his arm I need never know about it.'

I took the minaudière out of its case and set it on the table. Lot 24, it had been:

An Art Deco minaudière, of hinged cylindrical form, the exterior with black enamel and marcasite decoration, the interior with compact, mirror and *aide-mémoire*, and with inscription 'BUDAPEST 1934', with cord suspension, and tassel concealing a lipstick, in a fitted case.

Inside the case BARUCH, BUDAPEST was printed on the velvet in gold capitals. How had it arrived in London? Could it have belonged to a Jewish woman who left Hungary some time after 1934? Was she tall and elegant? Short and stout? Was her husband in business? This wasn't something a poor woman would have carried, she'd have had to have the clothes to go with it. Where were her frocks now? For that matter, where was she? I took the minaudière in my hands and closed my eyes as I'd seen clairvoyants do in films. It felt like another time, another life, but nothing came to me.

Nonetheless, I am in my small way a medium – I traffic in ghosts and the possessions, as often as not, of the dead. Almost all of the things I buy and sell were once in someone else's hands: necklaces from long-gone bosoms, rings from fingers long since departed in one way or another. And the punters, untroubled by ghosts, haggle. If I say, 'Fifteen pounds,' they look shrewd and say, 'Ten?' So I let it go for twelve; it cost me five.

Why had that man looked so failed? He wasn't memorable in any way except that.

Have you known anyone else with that look, Mrs Varley?
Objection!
Objection overruled. Witness will answer the question.
Well, yes, come to think of it, I have.
Would you name that person, please.
Giles Varley.
Any relation?
My husband. Late husband.
Thank you. Nothing further.

Giles had blue eyes, a face you could trust, a winning smile, and he worked hard. Bank managers pressed loans upon him and extended his overdrafts as he moved from one failure to another. I did my best to be a supportive wife; I propped him up as well as I could but it was like trying to build a tower out of wet dishcloths, and if I hadn't been stalling out regularly we'd have gone hungry. In all his ventures he had the necessary capital and skills and knowledge; he had everything except the knack of succeeding. He failed in antique clocks; he failed in stripped pine; he failed in picture-framing; he failed in loft-extensions but when he went into doll's houses he was quite successful until he found a way out with a bottle of sleeping tablets and half a bottle of Scotch. He left me with a house, a scattering of unpaid bills, and the conviction that if I'd tried harder he might have been a big man in doll's houses. Giles was a lovely man, really, but if there was one thing I learned from our nine years together it was that you can't turn a failer into a succeeder and you might as well not bother trying.

I felt doubly bereft when Giles was gone – propping him up had propped me up as well. Some weeks after his death I was in the V & A browsing in Chinese ceramics when I happened on my bat. 'Off my own bat, that's how I'll have to do it now,' I said to myself, and that's how I've done it ever since, with the tattoo to help me. Being alone is a lonely thing but that's all there is and in five hundred million years it won't really matter any more.

3

ROSWELL CLARK

Sometimes when people hear my name for the first time they give me strange looks or nod their heads knowingly and say 'Mmm hmm' or even 'Oh yes'. It was my father who chose that name for me. I didn't know it was anything out of the ordinary until I was nine, the year he died. I came home from school one day with a black eye and he asked me what happened. We were in our basement where the bulb over the work-bench in its green metal shade picked up the glitters and gleams of tools and a jumble of glass vessels and tubing. He was an inventor, and the place smelled of oil, metal, wood, rubber, Jack Daniel's (a bottle and glass are beside me as I write this; it has a wood-smoky smell and taste; it seems to me as I drink that the flavour is peculiarly American – long rifles; coonskin caps; 'D. Boon killed a bar on this tree in the year 1760') and something sharply chemical. I see him by the light of the green-shaded bulb, his face half in shadow; average height, average build; blue jeans, navy sweatshirt, sneakers. Brown hair, round face, glasses; he always looked surprised. He had a quiet and thoughtful way of speaking when he'd been drinking. 'What happened?' he said.

'George Kubat said you and Mom were aliens.'

'Who won?'

'I did. What's an alien?'

Dad heaved a big sigh. 'Roswell,' he said, 'back in 1947 there was something that happened at Roswell, New Mexico. People said they saw things – flying saucers. Then something crashed near there and they reported finding debris and the bodies of alien beings.'

'But what *are* alien beings, Dad?'

'Beings from outer space, from another planet. The government hushed everything up and said that nothing happened but a lot of people still think something *did* happen and it's been covered up.'

'And that's why you named me Roswell?'

'Well, I gave you that name because . . .' He seemed to have lost the rest of what he was going to say.

'Because what, Dad?'

'What, son?' He was leaning his folded arms on the work-bench and his eyes were closed. Sometimes he dozed off standing there like that.

'You were going to tell me why you gave me my name.'

'Yes. Because . . . Because you never know.'

'Never know what?'

'All kinds of things. Mysteries, life is full of them, whether it's UFOs or the Bermuda Triangle or whatever. And the government is always saying there's nothing out there.' He swept his arm to take in the whole basement workshop and knocked over the Jack Daniel's which was stoppered and didn't spill. 'Saying this is all there is.'

'You mean . . . ?'

'I mean this whole thing we call reality that you wake

up in every morning and go to sleep in every night. Not just the government, ordinary people too.'

'Ordinary people what?' It was hard to follow him sometimes.

'Only seeing what's in front of them or behind them. Just because the past is what it was doesn't mean the future can't be something else.'

I waited for him to go on but he didn't. I said, 'Is that why you named me Roswell?'

He went quiet and I thought he'd fallen asleep. Then he looked at me as if we were resuming a completely different conversation. 'It won't always be like this,' he said. He tapped a flask with some blue liquid in it and smiled at me. '"From this moment on,"' he sang quietly, '"no more blue songs, only whoop-dee-doo songs, from this moment on . . ."' Then he did fall asleep standing at his work-bench.

He was not a big success as an inventor; he often started out with something that led to something else that went nowhere. There was a self-winding hourglass. Why? I don't know but I remember what it looked like: the hourglass was supported by an arm that held the waist of it. When the sand ran into the bottom part the weight of it released a spring that flipped the hourglass over and wound itself up to do it again. After a while it ran down because of what Dad called 'the energy deficit'. 'If I could just lick that,' he said, 'I'd have perpetual motion.'

Mom came down to the basement looking for something just then. 'Perpetual bullshit,' she said.

My father owned the house but we never had much and I don't know what we'd have done if my mother hadn't always worked, mostly as a waitress. I had a newspaper route until I was old enough to work in the supermarket after school and on Saturdays. This was back in the sixties and Mom was a handsome woman then, fair-haired and taller than Dad, with blue eyes that seemed used to miles and miles of distance. Her maiden name had been Lindstrom and she looked like one of those pioneers who'd settled the Midwest, trailing a rope behind their covered wagons to help them steer a straight course through the tall grass of the prairies. Men liked to be waited on by her and tipped her well.

As soon as she got home from work she'd take her shoes off and put on a pair of fleece-lined slippers. Sometimes if she wasn't too tired she'd read to me, more often than not from her Bible which was bound in black leather with HOLY BIBLE stamped in gold on the cover and spine. It had what I thought of as a Presbyterian smell; if I closed my eyes I saw men in black with large hard hands and stiff collars. There was a blue ribbon bookmark and the type was good and black, the columns of text very strong, like verbal pillars to support the roof of faith. Sometimes the numbers of the verses seemed like eyes that watched me. I still have that Bible. On the flyleaf is written, in a firm and faithful hand:

Presented to our daughter Rachael
on her seventh birthday, March 21st, 1930
by Christian and Ursula Lindstrom

Favour is deceitful, and beauty is vain:
but a woman that feareth the Lord,
she shall be praised.
Proverbs, 31.30

Mom skipped around between the Old and New Testaments

when she read to me; she'd use a verse as a point of departure for a one- or two-minute sermon. I recall Matthew 5.13 – she was very intense when she did that one:

Ye are the salt of the earth: but if the salt have lost his savour, wherewith shall it be salted?

She always paused there. 'You hear that, Sonny? Remember that, and don't you lose your savour.'

'What's my savour, Mom?'

'Just remember the words – you'll understand them when you're older.'

Now and then for a special treat she'd read to me from *Grimm's Fairy Tales*; her favourites were 'The Goose-Girl' and 'Clever Elsie', both women who were hard done by. She read those not in her Bible voice but in a younger and more intimate way. When she did the part where Clever Elsie got turned away from her own house it gave me goose pimples.

Dad read to me sometimes too; he liked Andersen: his favourite was 'The Tinder-Box' in which the soldier ended up rich and married the princess. I could never understand how that soldier was able to lift the dog with eyes as big as the Round Tower in Copenhagen – that dog would have had to be at least as big as a house. 'I've given that a lot of thought,' said Dad. 'The soldier was down inside the hollow tree when he saw that dog, and because it was a magic place everything around the dog got bigger, the inside of the tree and the soldier too; that's how come he could lift it – he sort of grew into the job.' Dad's name was Daniel. If anyone asked him, 'As in the lion's den?' he answered, 'No, as in Jack.'

But I was talking about Mom. She hummed or sang when she was cooking and doing housework. Some were hymns and some were standards and there was one, a tune that she made up for Psalm 137 that she used to sing almost under her breath; sometimes she just hummed it: '"By the rivers of Babylon, there we sat down, yea, we wept, when we remembered Zion ..."' I don't recall that she ever got all the way through it. We were not a religious family but Mom sometimes turned to the Bible in the same way that Dad turned to Jack Daniel's.

'What's Zion?' I asked her. Dad was down in his workshop and we were alone.

She was ironing at the time, and she paused and blew out a little breath. 'Sonny,' she said – she always called me that when she was about to impart maternal wisdom. 'Sonny, Zion is where it was a whole lot better than it is now and you never get back there.'

'What are we supposed to do then?' I asked her.

She tilted her head to one side and looked at me across a few thousand miles of prairie. '"The ants are a people not strong,"' she said, '"yet they prepare their meat in the summer." Proverbs, that is; I forget the chapter and verse.'

'What does that mean, Mom?'

'It means that winter is always coming, and don't you forget it,' and she went back to the ironing.

Dad patented several things: in his notebook there were sketches and notes for a new kind of safety razor, magnetic buttonholes, and a self-cleaning comb. Mom told me that the razor had actually been made and sold but hadn't brought in much and was quickly superseded by a better one. Dad never got to develop all the ideas in the notebook. One rainy night in November after I was in bed but still awake I heard him go out and start the car. When everything was all right Dad was careless about the noise he made shutting the front door, but this time he left the house without a sound so I knew that he and Mom must have had an argument. Later I woke up when the police came to the door. They told Mom that Dad was dead: he'd wrapped his car around a tree while driving under the influence. He was forty-two years old.

Next morning I took his notebook off the work-bench, and when Mom asked me if I'd seen it I said no. I could read most of the words but I couldn't understand very much and there were numbers and symbols I couldn't make head or tail of. I hid the notebook in a cigar box in my sock drawer for when I got older.

Right after Dad's death my mother was on the phone a lot. A big man in a dark-blue suit came to the house, his aftershave was like a kick in the head; his eyes looked as if they'd been shot in with a rivet gun; you could tell from his smile that he enjoyed his work. He looked around at the furniture and the carpet and the wallpaper. He had a briefcase and he took some papers out of it, then Mom sent me out of the room while she talked to him. I listened at the door but they were too quiet for me to hear anything; I looked through the keyhole and saw Mom signing the papers.

After he left she just stood there looking out of the window. I asked her if that man was going to take away the furniture and she said no. Then I asked if he was the under-taker and she said no, there wasn't going to be a funeral. She told me that some people left their brains to science and Dad was doing that with his whole body. 'His brain too?' I said. I was thinking of all the ideas he had in his head, like perpetual motion; I was thinking of the words he hadn't said.

'Well, yes,' she answered, 'they're taking all of him.'

'What are they going to do with him?' I wanted to know. I wondered what kind of experiments they had in mind. I could see him high up on a platform in a thunderstorm where lightning would strike him.

'They'll do whatever scientists do,' she said, 'and he's bringing home more money this way than he did when he was alive, so be proud of your father. He finally achieved perpetual motion.'

'Is he in Heaven now?'

'I don't know where he is but it's just you and me from now on. He'll be missed at the liquor store but they'll have to stagger on without him.'

'I'll miss him too, won't you?'

'Oh yes, but, like they say, there is a Balm in Gilead.'

'Where's Gilead?'

'I'll let you know when I find it.'

The first I heard of what was really happening was that afternoon. I was out on our front walk killing ants with a hammer and Herbie Johnson came by. 'Are they going to let you watch when they crash-test your dad?' he asked me.

'What are you talking about?' I said.

'Don't you know? They're going to strap him into the driver's seat of a car and crash the car into a wall — they must figure he's got the experience for the job.'

'Don't come around here with that crazy kind of talk,' I said. 'I'll crash *you* into a wall.'

'My father works at Novatek,' said Herbie, 'and he's the one who told your mother they pay good money for dead bodies and they use them for dummies to test how safe a car is.'

That's when I punched him in the face and he went

home. And then I was left with Dad in my head singing 'From This Moment On' and smiling at me. Years later I bought a Frank Sinatra tape with that song on it but I always fast-forwarded past it. Psalm 137, though, that my mother used to sing to her own tune – I've got that on a CD with Boney M: 'Rivers of Babylon'. 'By the reevers of Bobby-lahn . . .' they sing, and they don't sound as if they're sitting down by the water – they're on a long dusty road and they're moving right along, going somewhere. I've got recordings of Psalm 137 by the choirs of King's College and Trinity College, Cambridge, Westminster Abbey, and Wells Cathedral, and they all sound like choirs in a church.

It was the summer of the last year of his life when Dad took me out to Cranbrook to see the Orpheus fountain by Carl Milles. We drove out there one afternoon, just the two of us. The heat waves were shimmering over Woodward Avenue and the smell of the upholstery in the car almost made me sick; when we got on to Lone Pine it was cooler because of the trees. We parked the car, walked through gates and an archway, went past a sculpture that I don't remember, then down some steps, along a promenade, up some steps and through some columns, and there it was: eight naked bronze figures, male and female, all in a circle around the spray that was coming up in the centre. The figures were realistic but smoother and simpler than real people and very athletic-looking. Some of them had their arms uplifted and some didn't; all of them seemed to be listening for something, listening so hard that their bodies stretched out and their arms and legs grew longer. All of them had one foot touching some foliage but that was only a support for the bronze; the figures were suspended in mid-air, suspended by their listening. One of the men was holding a bird in his right hand and with his left he motioned it to be quiet. The girl to his right had turned her face away and raised her hands, almost touching either side of her head as if she was saying, 'No, it's too much!' The listening seemed to go all the way up above the green of the trees to the blue sky and white clouds over us. There were mallard ducklings swimming in the fountain. The bronze looked cool; the water sparkled in the sun and a breeze was blowing the spray towards us. There was a smell of fresh-cut grass and flowers, purple ones that I didn't know the name of and yellow daisies. I heard birds in the trees. 'Remember,' said their voices, 'remember the listening of the bronze people.'

'What are they listening for?' I said to Dad.

'The music of Orpheus. He made such wonderful music that he almost brought his wife back from the dead.'

'Are these people dead?'

'I'm not sure.'

'Where's Orpheus?'

'He's not here.'

'Where is he?'

'I don't know.'

'Is one of the women his wife?'

'I don't think so. All that's here is his music and these people listening.'

I listened hard but all I heard was the whisper of the spray and the splashing of the water falling back into the fountain basin. 'I don't hear any music,' I said.

'The music is in the silence,' said Dad.

But I thought it must be very faint and far away from those eight in the fountain; they seemed to be trying hard to hear it, yearning for it to come to them. One of the men seemed to be saying, 'Louder!' with his arms up, both fists almost clenched as if he was trying to pull the music out of the air.

'I don't think they can hear it either,' I said to Dad. There was a sadness welling up in me that was almost choking me. 'They're trying but they can't hear it. Can you?'

'No.'

'But you said the music was in the silence.'

'It is but it's not music you can hear. You keep trying but you can't hear it. Maybe that's all there is.'

'All there is to what, Dad?'

'All there is to what I can tell you.' He rubbed the top of my head and gave me a hug. We had our cooler with us and we went and sat down on the lawn to eat our ham-and-cheese sandwiches and drink our drinks. Dad had his regular beer, Stroh's; I had a soft drink called Vernor's. I can almost remember the taste of it: sweet and gingery and the first swallow made you sneeze. While we ate and drank we watched the fountain people and the ducklings and the other visitors. That was the only time I ever saw the Orpheus fountain. Even after I was old enough to drive there myself I didn't; I was afraid I might not feel what I felt that time with Dad. It was something that I saved inside me.

After Dad died and then got smashed up again as a crash-test dummy I didn't do very well in school and I didn't feel much like talking to anybody. Mr Falco, the art teacher, gave me some clay and modelling tools. 'Maybe your fingers feel like talking,' he said. I tried to make a figure like the ones in the fountain but it wouldn't stand up; the legs gave way and the arms fell off. Mr Falco showed me how to make an armature, and then I did a figure of a man reaching for the music he couldn't hear. It wasn't very good but Mr Falco said it wasn't bad for a first time with clay.

I used to hang around the art room a lot, and as I got older the figures got better. When I was twelve I brought one home and showed it to Mom. 'What's that supposed to be,' she said, 'a basketball player?'

'He's reaching for music he can't hear,' I said.

'Aren't we all?' said Mom. 'I hope they're teaching you something useful at school; reaching for music you can't hear is not going to pay a lot of bills when you're older.'

Actually the figure wasn't all that good; none of them were and after a while I stopped making them. I didn't do any drawing or painting and I didn't hang around the art room any more. I was good at maths and algebra and when I got to high school I did well in chemistry. I kept reading Dad's notebook and I was understanding more of it all the time. There wasn't much else happening. I read a lot; I had a girlfriend for a while, her name was Pearl; she ditched me for a quarterback on the high-school team. I still had my part-time job at the supermarket. Mom was always talking about saving for the future but there wasn't a whole lot to save back then.

Finally the chemistry and the notebook began to pay off: in the high-school lab I produced a lump of malleable plastic but you couldn't do anything with it that you couldn't do with Silly Putty. In the notebook Dad had been trying out product names: Memoplast and Mnemoplast appeared several times so I knew I was looking for a plastic with a memory. I took over the basement workshop/lab and put in many hours there but it was slow going.

After graduating high school I got a job at Spectrum Displays in Eight Mile Road and worked my way up to making papier-mâché figures on chicken-wire armatures. Soaking strips of newspaper in flour-and-water paste and building up the forms on the chicken-wire was a restful and contemplative thing to do. The mixed-up bits of headlines gave me strange stories to think about: THREE DEAD IN STOLEN BASES AS INDIANS LOSE SENATE SUBCOMMITTEE. All human life was there in interesting variations, slowly assuming male and female form for Hallowe'en, Thanksgiving, Christmas, and other seasonal occasions. Sometimes they lifted their arms, sometimes not.

By the time I was in my twenties Mom had retired. She had two offers of marriage from men who seemed all right in their way but she didn't accept either of them. '"Vanity of vanities,"' she said to me. 'There's a time for gathering husbands and there's a time for having less bother.' She was heavily into Ecclesiastes around then and there was a new bottle of Jack Daniel's under the kitchen sink. Her faith in Jesus was no longer what it had been; she used to sing her own version of 'Just a Closer Walk with Thee': 'Thou art short but I am tall, Jesus, why are you so small?/ If you've got no help for me,/ Let it be, dear Lord, let it be.'

'You never used to be a drinker,' I said to her.

'Your father's name was Daniels, as in Jacks,' she said. 'Daniel, as in Jack. Or whatever. He died for my sins.'

'Who?'

'Your dad. I always put him down, never encouraged. Night he treed in the drove, drove in a tree, I told him . . .' She trailed off into silence but she was still awake.

'What did you tell him?'

'Told him he was a failure and I was sorry I married him. Crying when he left the house.'

'You or him?'

29

'Him. Not a good wife. He died for my sins. Jesus, why are you so small? Don't be like him, Sonny?'

'Like Jesus?'

'Like Dad. Be something, do something. My fault.'

I hugged her and said, 'Don't blame yourself,' but I knew I wasn't very convincing. With my arms around her I was remembering the Orpheus fountain at Cranbrook, the whisper of the spray and the droplets on the cool bronze.

I stayed on at Spectrum and I kept working on my basement chemistry. My mother needed more and more looking after as the years went by. When she was sixty-eight she had a stroke that paralysed her left side. At the hospital they did CT and MRI scans; they did EKGs and EEGs. Mom was looking very small. 'She's doing all right,' the neurologist told me. 'The brain does a surprising amount of self-repair. I think we'll see improvement in her speech and left-side mobility.'

'Ihha I, orihha ah I?' said Mom.

'Say again?' I said.

She said again and there was something familiar in the rhythm but she had to repeat it several times before I thought I recognised the Clever Elsie quote: 'Is it I, or is it not I?' was what Elsie said after she fell asleep in a field and woke up with a fowler's net and bells hung on her by her husband Hans. She was frightened and uncertain whether she was Clever Elsie or not. She went to her house but the door wouldn't open, so she knocked at the window and said to Hans, 'Is Elsie within?' 'Yes,' said Hans, 'she is within.' 'Ah, heavens!' said Elsie. 'Then it is not I.' She tried other doors but when they heard the jingling of her bells no one would open for her. Then Elsie ran out of the village and was never seen again.

'Is that it?' I asked Mom. 'Are you saying, "Is it I or is it not I?"'

She nodded vigorously and died.

She'd left instructions for her funeral; she'd asked for the simplest ceremony and that's what she got. She hadn't wanted anybody there except me so there were just the two of us and the minister. It was a grey November day, the deciduous trees black and bare after the first heavy rain of winter and the pines holding the chill and the wet. Among the surrounding tombstones were three angels, one of them turned towards us, two away. Crows in the pines looked on and quoted Ecclesiastes but the minister stuck to his text and insisted on the resurrection and the life. When he finished I read Psalm 137. The minister frowned when I got to the part about dashing the little ones against the stones but the crows called for an encore. The coffin was lowered into the grave and I threw a clod on top of it which just sounded like a lump of dirt hitting a wooden box. Shouting amongst themselves, the crows flapped away into the greyness and the minister and I departed while the gravediggers finished their work.

I hadn't cried during the burial service; I felt as estranged from my mother's death as I had from her life. When I went home I sat on our front steps and looked at the grass growing up through the cracks in the walk where I'd hammered the ants when my father died.

'You never know,' I said to the winter chill in the air. There was a row of new houses where there used to be trees; a man was working on his car in front of one of them. As I looked, the sky and the houses and the cars and the man all went flat, like wallpaper. It came to me, not for the first time, that I was a stranger in the country where I was born. I had friends whom I drank with and friends who invited me to dinner but sometimes it all seemed like TV with the sound turned off. I'd been reading Dickens and Trollope and a lot of British ghost stories. As I sat there under the grey wallpaper sky there came to mind the M. R. James story, 'Casting the Runes', and the slide show put on for the local children by Mr Karswell, in which

> . . . this poor boy was followed, and at last pursued and overtaken, and either torn to pieces or somehow made away with, by a horrible hopping creature in white, which you saw at first dodging about among the trees, and gradually it appeared more and more plainly . . .

There were other stories with London fogs, and newsboys running past the window shouting, 'Dreadful murder in the Marylebone Road!' while the landlord and his wife toasted a bit of cheese over a gas ring. Although I was well aware that the Victorian London of the stories was no longer to be found, England seemed a cosy place to me and I began to live there in my mind.

There was still work to be done in the basement but I was getting closer until finally, too late for my mother to see my success, I achieved Mnemoplast. I had a plastic that could be pushed, pulled, squeezed and crumpled but would return to the shape it had been cast in. As I worked in the basement I'd been trying to come up with a commercial application. I wondered what Dad would have done with it; I saw him dead and strapped into a car that crashed into a wall and then the idea came to me.

I patented Mnemoplast, then it took me a little over a year to get my design worked out and production set up but eventually I had my commercial application: Crash Test. It was produced and marketed by Merlin, Inc. for sixty-four-ninety-nine in the US and thirty-nine pounds ninety-nine pence here. It came in a glossy colourfully printed box and when you took it out of the box it felt good in the hand, not cheap. The battery-powered car was nicely detailed but of no recognisable make. When it hit whatever it was aimed at it crumpled and bits of it flew off as well as bits of the driver but it uncrumpled quickly and the loose bits of car and driver were easy to fit back on.

Crash Test appeared in US shops in October 1987, and though sixty-four-ninety-nine was a hefty price it quickly became the Christmas present that parents who couldn't afford it bought for their kids. The same thing happened when it came out here in November. The distributors had calculated correctly that a strong start in the US would cause a buying frenzy here at the later date. When stocks ran out in less than a month on both sides of the Atlantic there were auctions in which Crash Test changed hands at outrageous prices.

It isn't always easy to say why people do the things they do. I sold the house, moved to London, and bought a house in Fulham. I feel like a stranger here too but I *am* a stranger so it's all right. I married a woman I met here and maybe I'll say more about that later.

When I went to the V & A to look for the chair-cover bats I was a widower. By then I'd been living in London for eight years. Crash Test had been superseded by computer games and was barely ticking over in the US and UK although it was a little more lively on the Continent. I hadn't come up with any other commercial ideas or ideas of any other kind; I'd been drawing and painting a little: early on I'd found a life class and I made some OK sketches; I went water-colouring along the Thames; I did some oils also, a few nothing-special street scenes.

There came a time, however, when I had to put artistic development aside and give some serious thought to bringing in money. I'd reached a point where I really had to make something happen before too long when, early in 1999, Merlin forwarded a letter to me from Paris:

Dear Creator of Crash Test,

In the window of a shop I have seen Crash Test and immediately it draws me to itself. I see it demonstrated, see the dummy at the wheel knowing nothing, expecting nothing. The car starts up, not controlled by the dummy but by a hand above him, all-powerful. At speed it hurtles forward into a wall, CRASH! The car is smashed, the doors fly off, the windows also, the dummy's head, his arms, his legs! Alas! he is destroyed. But no, the all-powerful hand reassembles him, makes the car again like new, and once again Mr Dummy, who from experience has learned nothing, hurtles to his dismemberment.

I purchase the toy, I take it home where it comes out of its box as we come all new into the world. Now I am the all-powerful hand of Mr Dummy's destiny. CRASH! we go, and CRASH! again. 'Bravo!' I cry with vigour and enthusiasm. I applaud, I approve with delight your most profoundly metaphorical demonstration of the human condition. What are we all but dummies doomed to crash head-on into the death that speeds towards us? And for what are we being tested? Who can offer to this mystery an answer that will bear examination? No one! Yes, you have hit the eye of the bull with this so deep perception of *la comédie humaine*.

Please be so kind as to respond to this letter. I wish to commission privately works from you and I make to you the assurance that you will be well recompensed for the exercise of your most interesting talent.

With admiration and intense good wishes,

Adelbert Delarue

M. Delarue's address was in the Avenue Montaigne which made me think that he probably wasn't short of a franc or two. Eager to develop this promising connection, I wrote back and said that I'd be interested to hear what he had in mind. Within a week I had his reply with a cheque drawn on Coutts for five thousand pounds. His letter explained that this was a down payment for the work and that five thousand more would be coming my way on delivery.

He went on to describe what he wanted: a crash-dummy couple, 'man and woman anatomically complete, with functional parts and receptive orifices', engaged in sexual intercourse. The figures were to be thirty centimetres tall. They were not to be one composite unit but two independent dummies capable of assuming all positions possible for humans. They were to be 'electrically activated' and there was to be sound – he didn't specify what kind.

My first impulse was just to return M. Delarue's cheque but then I began to have second thoughts. In Crash Test I was showing a dummy being dismembered; how was that better than showing two dummies having a bit of fun? I could find no moral high ground so the question was simply how much the traffic would bear. I sent back the cheque and wrote that I couldn't do what he wanted for less than twenty thousand pounds, half of it payable up front. By return of post I got a cheque for ten thousand pounds and the go-ahead. Twenty thousand pounds for a bonking toy! Obviously he was some kind of a nutter but the cheque was good. I'd half expected him to back off when I upped the price but now if I kept the money this thing was going to be for real. I decided to keep the money, and from that moment on I had a patron. I was to let M. Delarue know when the figures were ready and he would send a courier to take delivery and pay me the other ten thousand pounds.

The dummy in my Crash-Test set was a coarse and primitive thing compared to what Adelbert Delarue wanted. Thirty centimetres seems a lot of room until you think of batteries and a motor of some kind, and these would have to be articulated bodies that might be doing the whole *Kama Sutra* for all I knew. And of course they'd be radio-controlled and I didn't want them to look like model cars with antennas sticking up out of them.

Then there was the matter of the 'functional parts'. My first thought was that the male member might as well be in a state of permanent arousal but then I imagined the figure in solitary repose on a desk or table flaunting its priapism so I decided to accept the challenge: zoom lenses got longer or shorter at the touch of a button and the booms of model cranes went up and down so presumably the thing could be managed somehow. As for the 'receptive orifices', they'd need a soft lining to prevent the dummies from sounding like an abacus. The audio tape could be in the base, worked by the remote radio control.

What was I going to make my figures out of? The Crash-Test dummies had been plastic mass-produced from my clay model, pretty much like Action Man although better articulated. But for twenty thousand quid M. Delarue was entitled to something a little more upmarket so I decided on wood; it was going to take a lot of time but I wanted my porno-dummies to be work I could be proud of. More or less. I could already imagine carving them and sanding them smooth. Before going to wood, however, I thought it best to do some trial-and-error on a clay model. At Green & Stone in Chelsea where I sometimes bought art supplies I was told that I'd find everything I needed at Tiranti's in Warren Street.

The day was grey but not yet showing its hand with any precipitation. I thought it might be a favourable greyness, it felt as if it was with me and not against me. Fulham Broadway station, excited by the attentions of workmen and machines, hummed in anticipation of the new self that would emerge from its chrysalis of scaffolding, hoardings, fluorescent tubing, and noise. Mid-morning, this was, and the platform not too crowded. The rails winced, a headlight appeared far back in the tunnel, gathered a Tower Hill train to itself in its onward rush, became large and loud, stopped, and slid its doors open. I boarded it, went to Embankment, and changed to the Northern Line.

When I came out at Warren Street there were red Jurassic earthmovers nodding and feeding behind the hoardings on the other side of Tottenham Court Road, their heads rising into view and dropping out of it again as two motionless cranes watched from a distance. I looked down Warren Street into a foursquare perspective of nothing in particular. 'What?' I said. Warren Street shrugged, and it began to rain, gently but perhaps with intent.

Undistracted by pubs, shops, cafés, and a health-food centre with free-standing sandwich boards that offered to restore the world's love life with Viagra, I proceeded to the modest blue shopfront of Est. 1895 ALEC TIRANTI LIMITED, TOOLS, MATERIALS & EQUIPMENT FOR MODELLING, CARVING, SCULPTURE. BOOKSELLERS Inside, exotic labels whispered siren music of haematite, jade oil and iron paste along with gilt cream, antiquing fluid, cupra, black patinating wax, gold leaf and rust remover. Elementary and advanced glues urged me to stick my world together; coloured waxes evoked the ghost of Benvenuto Cellini; unrolled canvas rolls of sharp and slender shapers hinted at undreamt-of subtleties of form; short and tall modelling stands in wood and metal beckoned tripodally; calipers in many sizes promised to transfer any measurement faithfully; and rows of carving mallets in beech and hardwood silently insisted on the verb, 'to thump'.

Ignoring everything but my immediate needs, I quickly acquired twenty-five kilos of terracotta clay, a nylon clay cutter, a tabletop modelling stand, two sliding armature supports, some armature wire, and a set of modelling tools. For the next stage, the woodcarving, I bought a book on how to do it, a variety of chisels, gouges, rifflers, fluters and veiners, beechwood handles as necessary, an oilstone, slipstones, honing oil, a buff hide leather strop, strop dressing, a small beechwood mallet, and a Scopas Chops, which was not a machine for decapitating sculptors but a kind of bench vice. Finally, with my Visa card breathing hard and myself in a state of wild surmise, I stepped out into the rain, found a taxi after a while, loaded my gear aboard, and went home.

I put the woodcarving equipment aside for the present and prepared for clay-modelling. New tools and materials have exciting smells; they smell as if good things are going to happen. 'Here goes,' I said. 'This is the first moment of the rest of my life.' I poured myself a large Jack Daniel's, said, 'Here's looking at you,' to whatever might be looking back, drank most of it, put the modelling stand on the work-bench, made the armature, cut off some clay, and started work on the female figure.

Although the traditional design of crash-dummies offers little scope for individuality I felt that liberties might be taken here and there; with the clay I could decide how far off straight I wanted to go, work out the articulation, and estimate my wood requirements. Both male and female faces would be blank and eyeless but the bodies could certainly help the body language along. The clay felt primeval under my hands; it smelled earthy and made me think of God and Adam. I watched my hands and was impressed by their confidence and skill. When I'd done both figures I must admit that I was pleased; the female was somewhat more voluptuous than the usual crash-dummy and the male was similarly robust; I was looking forward to seeing them in action.

I went to Moss & Co in Hammersmith for the wood. It was raining again that day; the greyness and the wet made the whole thing more private and I liked that. Moss & Co itself is rather private; it's in Dimes Place, a tiny alley you could easily miss, off King Street. Most of the north side of King Street between the Broadway and Dimes Place is taken up by Kings Mall Shopping Centre. Everything is nothing, it said brightly as I passed. Everybody is nobody. I averted my eyes and hurried on to Dimes Place.

I love specialist suppliers of all kinds – places that have exactly what you need and know all there is to know about it. Moss & Co have been around for a hundred and fifteen years, and not only are all the people somebody but all the woods are somebody as well. When you turn into Dimes Place you're in a long narrowness lined with sheds where long baulks of timber lean, each in their proper place with a sign on the shed saying what they are: iroko or jelutong or ebony, whatever. All the woods have their smells, sometimes very faint, like the ghost-breath of the trees they came from. When you look at all those straight and squared-off timbers you might not think of trees at first but in the sheds the forests gather round you, tall and shadowy, whispering wood. In the long narrow alley the paving stones glistened in the rain; the sounds of King Street were small and distant.

In the shed where the limewood was I put my hand on one of the timbers and closed my eyes. For a moment it seemed to me that I stood in an avenue of linden trees roofed in by dark leaves and branches that met over a dim perspective of shadowy trunks. There came to me the Schubert song, *'Der Lindenbaum'*, and with my hand on that wood I thought of Tilman Riemenschneider, the great fifteenth-century sculptor who worked mostly in lime. In the photographs in my books you can see his chisel marks on the faces of Christ and Mary and the saints.

I opened my eyes and I was back in Dimes Place and the whisper of the rain with my hand still on the wood. If I used lime I was connecting myself to that man who was, you might say, the Johann Sebastian Bach of woodcarving. Probably in his whole life he never got the equivalent of twenty thousand pounds for a single commission.

Stuart Duncan, one of the company directors of these ghostly forests, was in the office. I was half afraid that he'd ask me if I was qualified to use lime but when I told him what I wanted he said, 'You can probably find what you need right out here.' We went to the little room outside the office where there were remnants of various lengths and thicknesses. I found eight pieces that would give me more than I needed, all neat and smooth and blond.

On the way home on the Piccadilly Line I could see my chisels and gouges and hear the slithery rasp as I sharpened them on the oilstone. I felt wide-awake and excited. Odd, I thought, that I had never done any woodcarving. Why hadn't I? The hand, the eye, and the mind respond differently to different tools and materials. Once home, I put the wood on my work-bench and there it waited, whispering to itself.

Before I began the actual carving I needed to know how the figures were going to be made to work so I browsed the small ads in *Model World* and found Dieter Scharf, I CAN MAKE IT WORK – SPECIAL APPLICATIONS TO ORDER. He was local, too. I got some sketches and notes down on paper then I rang him up and went to see him the next day.

Scharf lived off the North End Road in Eustace Road, which today seemed somewhat sullen and withdrawn; the houses were looking at me the way the regulars look at you when you wander into the wrong pub. The sky was overcast, as it often is when I'm trying to find something. When I rang the bell the door was answered by a stern middle-aged woman in a flowered apron. She looked like a housekeeper in a horror film. 'He's in the basement,' she said. The house was dark and cool, the furniture was dark and brown; the curtains were drawn, the kitchen was silent.

Dieter Scharf's workshop was dark and cosy; it smelled of electrical wiring, oiled metal, and cheap cigars. A light bulb in a green metal shade looked down on various little engines and skeletal articulations that littered his work-bench; some looked as if they were arrested in mid-crawl or mid-hop, others were not that far advanced. Tools hung in their painted outlines on the wall. From this moment on, I thought: What? You never know.

Scharf didn't look like an indoor type; he was a short sturdy man with a brown weathered face, sudden blue eyes, and big strong hands. He might have been a charcoal-burner in a haunted forest, and although his basement was in SW6 it felt far away and elsewhere. He watched me as I took in his workshop. There was a sampler on the wall in a carved rustic frame; the stitches were in faded orange, pink, and mauve:

EGAL WIE MAN SICH DREHT,
DER ARSCH BLEIBT IMMER HINTEN.

'What does that say?' I asked him.

'"Whichever way you turn, your arse stays always behind." My grandmother gave me that.'

'Words to live by,' I said.

On a little box on the wall there was a small wooden figure of a horseman in medieval dress. About a foot to the right of the horseman was another little box with nothing on top of it. Between the two boxes and connected to them by wires was a pushbutton. 'This is Eustace Road,' said Scharf.

'St Eustace?' I said, pointing to the wooden horseman.

'Right.'

'But where's the stag?'

'Push the button.'

When I did that, St Eustace sprang from his horse and fell to his knees; the lid of the other box slid aside as a stag reared up, a tiny Jesus popped out of its head with his arms outspread between the antlers, and Bing Crosby sang 'White Christmas'.

'The music's a nice touch,' I said.

'Goes pretty good, I think,' said Scharf. 'There never was a St Eustace.'

'Just as well for him and his family; in the story they ended up being roasted alive in a brazen bull.'

'This will teach us not to talk to strange stags. Have you an interesting problem for me?'

'I think so.' I showed him my sketches and explained my requirements.

Scharf laid the sketches on his work-bench and perused them, humming '*Der Lindenbaum*' the while.

'How come you're humming that?' I said.

'It's one of those songs that's often in my head, it's a goodbye song – he's saying goodbye to his youth, his dreams, his hopes. The rustling of the branches speaks to him, offering rest; but for him there is no rest as off he goes on his winter journey. No rest for any of us, not?'

'I guess not.'

He drummed on the sketches with his charcoal-burner's fingers. 'Someone has commissioned you to make this?'

'Yes.'

'You'll do anything for money, yes?'

'I'll do a lot of things for money.'

'I also. Have you met this person who commissions you to do this?'

'No.'

'What, a letter comes out of nowhere?'

'Yes.'

'Then a cheque?'

'Yes.'

'Wonderful.' He spread out the sketches and lit one of his foul cigars. 'You want both figures to be active, yes?'

'Yes.'

'In any position and independent of a base?'

'Yes.'

'So for this we need radio control. There must be an aerial on each one and I think you don't want the sort that sticks up as on a model car.'

'No.'

'We can do internal ones if the distances are short. Probably these are for indoor use, not?'

'I doubt very much he'd be taking them outdoors.'

'So internal is OK then. You want the whole articulated torso to be motorised or only the pelvis?'

'Pelvis only – the articulation will allow the rest of the torso to move with it.'

'Arms? Legs?'

'They'll stay in the position they're put in except as the pelvis moves them.'

'Your sketch indicates that his pimmel elevates and extends – a commanding member, this one.'

'Well, you know, this whole thing is what it is.'

'I can make it work. You want the batteries in the thighs?'

'That's what I'm hoping. Will that be a problem?'

'No, we can do this. Let me make my calculations, and if you phone me tomorrow I can tell you how much this will cost.'

We said our goodbyes; I made my way through the cigar smoke and walked home thinking about Adelbert Delarue. Twenty thousand pounds for a bonking toy! What kind of man would pay that kind of money for such a thing? Obviously someone who had money to throw around, and he'd turned up at a time when I needed money. This whole thing began to feel like something fated. Not for the first time I tried to visualise M. Delarue: sometimes I saw him alone and scholarly in a booklined study; sometimes in action with a partner while watching my crash-test dummies. Occasionally St Eustace and company got into the picture; Eustace leapt off his horse, the stag reared up; Jesus popped out of its head and watched while the dummies did their thing and M. Delarue and partner (frequently a stern housekeeper) did theirs.

When I got home I worked out how to get the necessary parts out of my blocks of lime, then I made drawings, transferred them to the wood, clamped the first block in the Scopas Chops, picked up chisel and mallet, and got started on the male torso. The mallet blows and the bite of the chisel sounded good to me; as the shavings fell away from my blade I felt hooked-up, connected, and it occurred to me that this might be how artists felt. In six weeks my figures were ready for Dieter Scharf. The drilling and carving for the motor, battery, and wiring spaces had been ticklish but although I'd bought enough wood to allow for errors and wastage I hadn't made any errors and I'd wasted nothing.

Dieter Scharf charged me twenty-five hundred pounds for radio controls and aerials, motors and installation. I painted the quartered yellow-and-black discs on the dummies and varnished them. The smooth hardness of the lime and the polished surfaces heightened the anatomical hyperbole so that even side by side in repose the figures had a beguiling lewdness. When the male dummy zoomed into readiness and the female received him they did what they were designed to do; their blind and expressionless faces radiated a mystic calm while their lower parts worked tirelessly. The primary receptive orifice, lined with foam rubber, maintained a discreet silence as the pelvises kept up a quiet clacking that was as cosy as the tick of a kitchen clock. I put a Walkman mechanism and two little speakers in the base, the top of which was upholstered like the back seat of a car. The audio was car-crash sound effects, and I looped the tape so that the noise was continuous. When I had the whole thing put together with the dummies bonking and the sound crashing I showed it to Dieter and he said, 'There we have it – dummy sex on a road to nowhere.'

I faxed M. Delarue and he replied that I was to send the radio controls, described as being for models, via DHL. The base was to go the same way, described as a customised Walkman. The figures would be collected by his personal courier the next afternoon. At about three o'clock that day a very large man with a shaven head appeared at my door. He had a big smile, several gold teeth, and an unbroken nose; my guess was that the other man's nose was normally the one to get broken. He was about seven feet tall and carried a Louis Vuitton holdall. His suit was expensive but his wrists and hands came out of the sleeves in a grappling sort of way. 'I am Jean-Louis, arrived by Eurostar,' he said. 'Me, I am ready to roll.' His taxi stood waiting.

'Do you watch a lot of American TV?' I said. '*Hill Street Blues* repeats?'

'You got it. I come from M. Delarue. Here is ID, also message.' He pulled out a wallet and showed me a driver's licence which identified him as Jean-Louis Galantière.

'Nice name,' I said.

He shrugged. 'It goes.'

The note from M. Delarue confirmed that my visitor was who he said he was and would give me a cheque for twenty thousand pounds as soon as he received the figures from me. Ten thousand of this was a down payment on a new commission: a crash-dummy mastiff for which he was again offering twenty thousand pounds. The mastiff was to have the usual fully functional parts and was to be made to the same scale as the male and female dummies.

'OK?' said Jean-Louis, looking at his watch. 'We are burning daylight, pardner.'

'You like John Wayne?'

'In my book he is Number One. With him no one takes liberties. You give me merchandise, I give you money, I am out of here, yes?' He opened the Louis Vuitton and let loose a powerful aroma of dirty socks. 'My cover,' he explained. 'The *douanier* looks not too close.'

'Are you sure you'll get through Customs all right?'

'No problem. I am as one invisible.'

'You're a whole lot of invisible,' I said.

'Rest you tranquil – it goes.'

I removed the batteries from the figures and put them in a small bag which I gave Jean-Louis with the written operating instructions. 'What an *équipement*,' he said when he saw the male figure.

'Life is short but Art is long,' I replied.

He wrapped each figure separately in dirty socks, put them into hidden side compartments in the Louis Vuitton and closed it. He gave me the cheque and we shook hands. '*Au revoir*,' he said.

'*Au revoir*. Would you like something before you go? One for the road?'

'Have you perhaps the Jack Daniel's? A small one only.'

I fetched the bottle and two glasses, and poured us both large ones, confident that M. Delarue could afford the taxi's waiting time. '*Santé*,' said Jean-Louis as we clinked glasses.

'Here's looking at you,' I returned. 'Are you just a courier or do you do other work for M. Delarue?'

'I am his chauffeur.'

'What sort of a man is M. Delarue?'

'Rich,' he answered, then made a gesture of zipping his lips, after which he raised an admonitory index finger.

'Right, no more questions about him. What did you do before you became his chauffeur?'

'Time.'

'Ah.' I was going to ask him what he did the time for but thought better of it, so we drank companionably but without conversation from then on until he left, and thus ended the first transaction with my new patron.

The next morning a fax arrived in which M. Delarue said that he was delighted, his satisfaction was greater than expected; the action of the figures together with the sound produced an experience without parallel. He was lost in admiration and looked forward with eager anticipation to the mastiff.

It's astonishing, really, how quickly the strange becomes the usual. Whoever and whatever M. Delarue was, he was willing and able to pay handsomely for his playthings and I now settled into the role of providing him with the wooden objects of his desire. As I began my mastiff research I wondered what the end of all this would be. In the meantime, craftsmanship and the moral obligation to do the job right took over. As well as something else which I've already touched on: these wooden erotica excited me; not only erotically but – dare I use the word? – artistically. Working with wood felt good; it put new heart into me. I was beginning to feel like an artist, beginning to wonder what I might carve when I finished with M. Delarue's commissions.

I looked at mastiffs in books, I talked to mastiff breeders on the telephone, I went to Watford to photograph a dog called Longmoor's Dark Dandy and paid his owner fifty pounds. Remarking my interest in the animal's private parts, he smiled knowingly and asked for twenty-five pounds more, which I paid with a cryptic smile. Although he obviously had theories, I very much doubted that he could imagine what my research was for.

On my return I bought more wood, made my clay model, just a little hyperbolised, went to the lime, thoroughly enjoyed the carving, and ended up with a crash-dummy mastiff that could confidently collide with the best society.

As before, Dieter Scharf supplied the pelvic motor. 'It didn't take us long to get down on all fours, did it,' he said.

Although no sound had been requested I looped a tape of Maria Callas singing '*E strano! E strano!*' and the aria that follows in Act One of *La Traviata*, '*Ah, forse e lui che l'anima . . .*', 'Ah, perhaps he is the one . . .' The finishing touch on my crash-dummy creatures was always the yellow-and-black-quartered discs; these came to have an almost mystical quality for me, particularly when they were in motion.

Jean-Louis and I did the business as before, and Bonzo was received as enthusiastically as the first figures had been. 'The animal is all that one could wish,' wrote M. Delarue, 'and the music – what a touch!' The cheque Jean-Louis had given me brought the total up to fifty-five thousand pounds, fifteen thousand of which was a down payment on the next commission. 'It is my hope,' he wrote, 'that your earnings from these commissions will gain for you a little non-commercial time in which to follow your art wherever it leads.'

My art! Although I was beginning to feel like an artist I hadn't been thinking of what I did as art but perhaps a rethink was in order. This was a time when unmade beds and used condoms were fetching high prices, and certainly my crash-dummies were no less – maybe even more – art than those.

M. Delarue's next request was for a crash-dummy gorilla with the usual specs. Feeling that he might have underpaid me on the first two commissions, he was offering thirty thousand pounds, confident that my work, as always, would exceed expectations. That would bring the total up to seventy thousand pounds for my art. Maybe with a capital A: my Art. A crash-dummy gorilla, OK. Having done the others, I found no reason to draw the line at this one. But what did he want from me besides his crash-dummy bonking menagerie? What was he expecting me to do with this time that his money was buying for me?

Never mind, I said to myself, just make a good gorilla. I decided not to visit the Regent's Park Zoo. When I last went there, some years ago, there was a female gorilla licking her urine off the floor. Was that her way, I wondered, of saying, 'Is it I or is it not I?' I had *National Geographics*, I had a video of David Attenborough whispering his narration while chewing vegetation and hanging out with a silverback and his troupe; and I had my own idea of gorilla-in-itself, a creature likely to be the dominant member in any relationship. I rigorously maintained my standards and eventually achieved a wooden gorilla with whom a wooden woman might crash any party of the appropriate scale with complete assurance.

I thought of my gorilla woodenly dreaming of African mountains while doing what I'd been paid to make him do. I gave Jean-Louis a tape to take with him for the gorilla-and-partner soundtrack: : Bach's *Passacaglia and Fugue in C Minor.* I couldn't find a recording by Marie-Claire Alain on that wonderful organ in Flensborg, Sweden that sounds as if it was made from the salt-encrusted timbers of Noah's Ark so I went with Albert Schweitzer at the Parish Church in Gunsbach, Alsace. On reflection I was pleased with that choice; I thought Schweitzer and the gorilla would get on well together.

4

SARAH VARLEY

You can do it either way, really: Monet defined his forms with light; Chardin with darkness. Monet's figures, his flowers, his rocks, his boats and his sea all partake of the light; they mingle with it; one can't say exactly where the light leaves off and they begin. Chardin's people, his animals alive and dead, his still lifes all husband carefully the light allotted to them in the darkness that defines them. Chardin died in 1779, Monet in 1926. Certainly Monet's is the more modern approach but I am a Chardin sort of person. At the exhibition at the Royal Academy I stood in front of his paintings caught by the lucent mystery of a glass of water, the quiet crucifixion of a hare. No, I am not modern.

In my buying and selling I'm closer to the modern era; I've got Clarice Cliff and Susy Cooper china, Kosta and Orrefors glass. In costume jewellery I've got two Schiaparelli, three Trifari and one Kramer at present, a few things that go back to the twenties and earlier but mostly they're from the forties and fifties: coloured glass, marcasite, paste. I like cheerful things that sparkle and I like to see women smiling as they put them on.

Saturday went well at Chelsea Town Hall. I bought almost

as much as I sold but they were things I expect to do all right with. I had the usual timewasters who blocked the stall without buying anything but nothing was stolen and there was a really nice Japanese woman who appreciated what I had on display and bought two of my most expensive necklaces. It isn't just the money, it's the recognition I crave – the little smile and nod and the look that says, 'Ah yes, you know what's good.'

On Mondays I do Covent Garden, the Jubilee Market, so on Sunday I look at my stock and decide what to take; it's the sort of thing that tends to fill the time available for it. I was luxuriating in indecision when the doorbell rang and I knew it would be Jehovah's Witnesses. I hadn't seen any for a long time and I'd begun to wonder whether they were an endangered species. These two looked diffident but daring, like animals returning to an old habitat but taking nothing for granted. One was a white man, slight and bespectacled, who looked like a stamp collector. He was wearing a suit and a tie. The other was a black woman, tall and delicate, soberly dressed, who seemed remote but committed. They stood on the doorstep, prepared for rejection but modestly hopeful.

'Good morning,' I said.

'Good morning,' said the man, looking slightly more confident. 'We're going round encouraging people to read the Word of God and take comfort and guidance from it.'

'I've read the Old Testament and the New Testament and the Apocrypha,' I said. 'I made notes at the time but I can't give you chapter and verse.'

'So you don't turn to the Word of God regularly?' said the woman, gently but with a little edge to it.

'No. What's your message for the present time?'

'This is a time of adversity, isn't it?' said the man. 'I

mean, look around you – is this what you'd call a good time?'

'No, it isn't.'

'It isn't; it's a time of adversity and this is God's answer to a world that has turned away from Him. Do you remember Daniel 2. 44?'

'No.' The sun was doing its Sunday-afternoon thing: five hundred million years left to live. Peter Rabbit on Mars?

'. . . kingdoms,' said the man. The woman nodded.

'What?' I said.

'Nebuchadnezzar's dream, Daniel 2.1,' said the man. '"His spirit was troubled, and his sleep brake from him."'

'I remember Belshazzar's feast but not Nebuchadnezzar's dream.'

'Nebuchadnezzar,' said the man, 'had a dream in which he saw a great image. "This image's head was of fine gold . . ."'

'That's the one with feet of clay,' I said. 'Right?'

'Right,' said the man. He took out his little Bible in which the passage was underlined. 'Daniel 2.42,' he said triumphantly. '"And as the toes of the feet were part of iron, and part of clay, so the kingdom shall be partly strong, and partly broken." And in the next verse: "And whereas thou sawest iron mixed with miry clay, they shall mingle themselves with the seed of men: but they shall not cleave one to another, even as iron is not mixed with clay."'

'Yes,' I said, 'but I don't remember what's next.'

'Now we come to it,' he said, 'Daniel 2.44: "And in the days of these kings shall the God of heaven set up a kingdom, which shall never be destroyed: and the kingdom shall not be left to other people, but it shall break in pieces and consume all these kingdoms, and it shall stand for ever." That's God's Kingdom, and Jesus is its King.'

'Not Jehovah?'

'No, Jehovah appointed Jesus King in 1914.'

'And he's been King ever since,' said the woman.

'He's doing a lot better than Prince Charles, isn't he,' I said.

Both of them looked at me with their heads at a slight angle. 'Well,' said the man, 'it's been a pleasure talking to you. Can we leave this brochure with you?' There was a tri-ethnic group of faces on the cover. *What Does God Require of Us?* was the title, correctly spelled.

'Thank you,' I said. 'The blood is the life, isn't it?'

'Sorry?' said the man.

'The blood is the life, isn't it?'

'That's what God says.'

'Dracula said the same thing. That's why Renfield ate flies. What about the Jehovah's Witness who lost five pints of blood in a machete attack? Did you see it in *The Times*?'

'We heard about it.'

'Why don't Jehovah's Witnesses accept blood transfusions?'

'It says right here,' said the man, opening the brochure to the appropriate page, '"We must not take into our bodies in any way other people's blood or even our own blood that has been stored (Acts 21.25)."'

'Hang on,' I said. I went and got my King James version off the shelf and looked up Acts 21.25. Returning to my visitors I read aloud: '"As touching the Gentiles which believe, we have written and concluded that they observe no such thing, save only that they keep themselves from things offered to idols, and from blood, and from strangled, and from fornication." That isn't what I'd call a clear-cut prohibition of transfusions,' I said.

'Jehovah's requirement is in those words,' said the man, 'and Jehovah's Witnesses obey it.'

'But this bloke,' I said, 'renounced his Jehovah's Witnesshood because the blood is the life and he wanted a transfusion so he could go on living.'

'Not everyone has the faith to uphold God's laws,' said the man smoothly. 'Thank you for your time and your interest. We must be going.' And they went, still with their heads at an angle. The brochure had a back-of-a-cereal-box quality but obviously it works for the people who go around ringing doorbells to share their enlightenment with the rest of us. If there were a Jehovah, it's just the sort of thing he might do as an audience warm-up for Armageddon. I *am* actually a believer: I have faith that there's nothing that cares about us one way or the other.

After the Jehovah's Witnesses left I went out to the garden where I grazed safely on the *Sunday Times* and the *Observer* and drank many cups of lemon tea. The usual blackbird, the husband, was standing on the fence and zicking to his wife and children. I think they may be nesting in the camellia bush which is too low to be safe but I haven't wanted to disturb them by getting close enough to see. It's such a peaceful sound, that zicking; it reminds me that the seasons still arrive at their appointed times, more or less.

I was much impressed by the daring of a forty-four-year-old woman (my age exactly) of whom there were several photographs in the *Sunday Times*. Her boyfriend had spent two years and three thousand pounds building a medieval siege engine, a trebuchet – a big one with a one-tonne lead counterweight. The idea was to use it for hurling people one hundred and twenty feet through the air into a safety net. The thing had been tested with crash dummies and by the boyfriend whose trajectory went as planned. Both the woman and the boyfriend (fifteen years younger) are members of the Dangerous Sports Club. A portrait photo showed her before the slinging looking about as worried as I'd look in that situation. Not that I'd ever allow such a thing to happen.

In the event she flew through the air as planned but when she landed in the safety net she bounced out, fell thirty feet to the ground, and broke her pelvis. I kept going back to the photo of her before she became a human missile. Dread was the only word for the expression on her face as she weighed one thing against another. 'She was shaking with fear,' the boyfriend was quoted as saying. She was in a stable condition in hospital, according to the *Sunday Times* report. I imagined her watching when the crash-dummy did what she was planning to do. I saw it hurtling through the air in a graceful parabola, its yellow-and-black discs making its flight easy for the eye to follow. I imagined the conversation with her boyfriend:

BOYFRIEND: *See, it hits the net every time. Same weight as you, approximately same body mass — can't miss.*

WOMAN: *Your calculations worked out all right, I can see that. And it worked perfectly when you did it.*

BOYFRIEND: *You don't look comfortable with it. Look, you don't have to do this. We needn't do every single thing the same.*

WOMAN: *No, I want to do it, I really do. It's one of those things I have to do.*

BOYFRIEND: *But you look scared and you're shaking.*

WOMAN: *You know how I am – I shook before all of our*
            bungee jumps too.
BOYFRIEND: *OK, if you're sure.*
WOMAN: *I'm sure.*

Her face haunts me. I wonder if she and the boyfriend are still together.

At 4.30 Monday morning it's still really Sunday night. I woke up from a dream in which I arrived at the platform just as the train was pulling out. I ran as fast as I could but I wasn't fast enough. So I was awake before the alarm went off; it was only ten minutes to four. I tried without success to get back to sleep, finally rolled out of bed at half-past feeling hard done by, had breakfast, did my nervous trips to the loo, put on my rucksack that almost drives me into the ground every time, slung a shoulder bag almost as heavy, and trundled my bursting trolley bag out into the foredawn.

It had rained Sunday night, so there was a little freshness in the air. As I came out of Doria Road into the New Kings Road the birds were pretending that the world was new and the sky held that very delicate innocent blue that only early risers see. The Green Café and Delicatessen showed no signs of life except the rubbish bags heaped on the pavement. Phase 8's window was an exercise in boredom – all beige skirts and tops, hardly a strong start for the week. Jenesis was better, all mauve and vigorously so. The Candles shop, offering picnic hampers and other things in wickerwork, also displayed candles of various kinds and maintained its identity in a world of change. Shopkeepers have an obligation, I think, to display their wares in a way that will give the early and late passersby something to go on with.

Starbuck's Coffee had a cosy night light going but was still not open; the Fulham E-Bar with its nocturnal blue neon was obviously not awake at 5.00. At the corner of Parsons Green Lane I nodded to the two telephone boxes that stood like a pair of lanterns and paused to acknowledge the trees which were still embracing the night. I admire those trees; fashions come and go but the trees still maintain their original identity, their unfashionable mystery. They hold last night's darkness like lovers reluctant to let go.

As I walked, the sky lost its innocent blue and paled towards the reality of Monday morning. St Dionis Church and Mission Hall, Headquarters of the Second Fulham Parsons Green Scout Troop and the Second Fulham St Dionis Girl Guide Company, approached and receded. Sometimes I am astonished that there should be buildings built and institutions maintained to string out the brevity of human life over successive generations; trees don't do that, they just hold on to the darkness and accept the light night after night and day after day without pretensions to permanence.

The Freedom Brewing Company, the Chairs place, Wurtford Solicitors . . . Very good: one downs a pint, sits in a chair, draws up a will, and proceeds to Co-operative Funeral Services, where a man in Bermuda shorts was co-operating with two bulging and heavy dustbin bags. And the day hadn't even begun. The Civilised Car-Hire Company probably offered transport to and from funerals but I trundled on to the tube station, took a deep breath, negotiated the turnstile and heaved self and impedimenta step by step up the stairs to the platform which commanded a view of Parsons Green, St Dionis Church, and the hunting grounds of Harrington Lowndes Estate Agents: ANY OTHER CHOICE COULD BE DISAPPOINTING. Oh dear.

Every day is so full of large and small choices and I make so many wrong ones.

5

ADELBERT DELARUE

Always it is interesting, is it not? to look rearward from the present moment to those earlier present moments from which it has arisen. If one perspicaciously from effects to causes traces the development of anything, one sees with clarity how infallibly one thing leads to another. And yet sometimes it is easier from the present to look forward and predict an outcome than it is from an outcome to look backward and determine a cause. But at every moment of every day and in the night as well, like newly hatched turtles racing to the sea, causes are hurrying to their effects. To me it seems that each of us is the effect of past causes and the cause of new effects.

And who am I? Herewith I introduce myself: Adelbert Delarue at your service, patron of the arts and champion of the insufficiently recognised. The events of this history have in these pages not yet run their course but in reality they are already in the past and I have been asked to make my small but I hope useful contribution.

May I speak briefly of guilt? Who is there without it? Guilt can be inherited like money and I have been living comfortably on the interest of what was left to me. One makes one's arrangements. My name was not in the beginning

Delarue, no. I was christened Adelbert von Peng. Ha ha, what a funny name. Peng means bang in German, and my father was Ludwig von Peng who was, three guesses, yes? a munitions maker. Ho ho. Such fun. From these roots a little distance is not a bad thing, is it? My fortune is discreetly deployed in many places: I don't even know where all of it is but I employ those who do the deploying and they know where to find it.

Art! What is there more wonderful? From the acorn grows the oak and from talent comes maybe a real artist who from nothing makes something, who from here, there, out of the air, plucks an idea that takes us all to a place where we never before have been. Crash-dummies, what a conception, truly. What a metaphor.

6

ROSWELL CLARK

It was a day full of bright sunlight, the kind that makes you blink when you come out of a cinema matinée with nothing but reality ahead of you. I was standing in front of the Fulham Tattoo Centre. Jesus, I thought, is this really me about to go into a tattoo parlour? Although beautiful young models and other sleek and chic people now sport tattoos, often in places somewhat off the beaten track, I am old enough to associate tattoo parlours with drunken sailors, neon signs with missing letters, and pawnshops offering knuckle-dusters and flick knives. It isn't like that now: nothing nocturnal, the Fulham Tattoo Centre stood in the respectable broad daylight of the Fulham Road between a continental grocer and a launderette. Writ large on the windows in red outlined with yellow were the words TATTOO, BODY PIERCING, and the telephone number. Body piercing, I reflected, has been celebrated by Christianity for centuries in paintings and sculpture and I have seen Sacred-Heart tattoos from time to time. Peoples with other gods do both and turn up in *National Geographic*.

WARNING, said a sign in the window:

NO
PERSON TATTOOED
UNDER THE
INFLUENCE OF
DRINK OF DRUGS.

Inside there were further admonitions:

IF YOU ARE IN
A RUSH DON'T
EXPECT ME
TO BE.
A GOOD
TATTOO
TAKES TIME
TO DO.

And:

TATTOOS LAST
A LIFETIME, SO
MAKE SURE YOU
GET THE BEST.

A lifetime! What about me? Was I going to last a lifetime? The tattoo would have to take its chances with me.

The walls were decked with dragons, devils, daggers, hearts, flowers, skeletons, Chinese ideographs and abstract repeat patterns that you might see in a typographic catalogue. There was a display case containing a variety of ornaments meant to be attached to or passed through the wearer's flesh.

There were large colour photographs of a naked oriental woman whose body was completely covered with what appeared to be either one long story or a series of colourful abstractions. My attention was diverted by two young black women, one tall and pretty, the other short and plain, both with studs in their noses. They were perusing floral designs.

'Where?' said the pretty one.

'Where would you do it?' said the plain one.

'Here.' She put her hand just above the pubic area. 'What about you?'

'I'd do mine a little higher up,' said the plain one.

A large white man with a broken nose came in. He was wearing a T-shirt, had a Union Jack on his right arm and nothing on his left. He stood for a while in front of a red devil design, then left looking thoughtful. SOOTTAT, said the red-and-yellow letters on the window as I looked out. This is all there is, said the Fulham Road.

'Mr Clark,' said Mick Corbett, the tattoo artist, as he emerged from that part of the studio where the work was done, 'I'm ready for you now.' A tall man in his thirties, serious-looking, he had a very small dark moustache and a beard that was little more than a chin-outliner; the close-cropped receding hair on top of his head was equally minimal. I'd asked him earlier how he came to take up tattooing.

'My older brother had tattoos,' he said, 'and I wanted to get tattooed too but I was only twelve then and I was too young. When I was fifteen I went back and got a tattoo and after that I kept coming in for more until they were sick of the sight of me. They said, "Why don't you save up and get the tools and learn how to do it yourself?" So I did and it took me five years before I was ready to do it for money.'

'Where did you go to learn it?' I asked him.

'I just practised on myself and my friends for the first three years.'

'On yourself!'

'Yes. Most tattoo artists have terrible-looking legs because that's where you practise when you're learning. You put your leg up on a chair and it's easy to work on.'

His arms were illustrated so copiously that the designs merged in a jungle of pattern and colour from which faces, or perhaps not, peeped indistinctly. I followed him into the STRICTLY PRIVATE area and we went into a little fluorescent-lit room that looked very medical: a white enamel instrument table, glass shelving for more instruments and a tall shelf unit for coloured inks. An Anglepoise lamp gave additional light to a towel-covered arm rest; I'd given him a photo of the bowl with my bat a couple of days ago and he'd done an enlarged copy of the bat on tracing paper. Laying the tracing on carbon paper with the carbon side up he'd gone over the outline to prepare the tracing for transfer to my skin.

He put on latex gloves, sprayed my shoulder with antiseptic liquid, then shaved it, went over it with an alcoholic stick, and applied the transfer. When he lifted the tracing paper there was the dark-blue outline of my bat, about two and a quarter inches from wingtip to wingtip. After a few minutes for drying there was more antiseptic, then Vaseline to lubricate the skin. He prepared the disposable caps for the two inks, a light red and a dark red, and dipped the outlining machine into the dark red. Then I placed my arm on the arm rest, the gleaming little machine buzzingly approached my shoulder, the needle pricked my skin, and the eighteenth-century bat of the Yongzheng period taxied down the runway into the new century on me. Would it get me off the ground? I was paying for the tattoo but was I a legitimate passenger or a stowaway?

Before this I hadn't put my tattoo thoughts into words with any precision; I felt that in being tattooed I was offering myself to some unknown chance of luck; but now it came to me with simple clarity that I just wanted that bat to take me aboard and fly me out of where I was in myself.

When I'm in a pub with a few drinks in me I can talk more or less freely to strangers but I don't like to lay out my whole history for everybody and it isn't easy for me to type it out here. I'll say what I can and maybe more at another time. At my present age of forty-seven my back story is not an album of happy memories. I was married for seven years; Jennifer died in a car crash in 1995. After that I kept mostly to myself for the next few years: I did some painting and drawing, some reading. I watched a lot of videos, went to museums and concerts, lived from day to day the best I could. I'd nothing much to say to anyone; I got fewer and fewer dinner invitations and became more and more boring to myself. But after a while I was ready to move on to whatever was next and that's when I decided on a bat tattoo and met Sarah Varley. That encounter at the V & A was the sort of thing that sometimes leads to a closer acquaintance but I didn't feel like starting with a new person; there was still too much unfinished business in my head.

Adelbert Delarue was much in my mind of course. He was delighted with the gorilla and particularly with the Bach tape. 'So austere!' he wrote. 'This so noble primate with his grandeur priapic, how he resonates and echoes lost evolutionary memories while the music goes up and down and in and out with him. To this I respond with my whole heart and *membrum virilis* also. With a friend I watch this moving art of yours and we find in it always new stimulation and new things to think about deeply. Those black-and-yellow discs, the eroticism of them! Life, what is it? Motion, to where does it take us? "*Ou sont les neiges d'antan?*"'

His cheque had arrived with his letter. A few weeks passed with no further word. Then one day another letter arrived:

My dear Roswell,

These so powerful works that you have executed for me have been a source of great satisfaction to me and I hope to you also. My friend and I (her name is Victoria Fawles and with her I improve my English) amuse ourselves with these creatures of wood and we with grease paint apply to ourselves the black-and-yellow discs of dummyhood. A carnival of strange sensations – who can define the boundaries of pleasure? My commissions are of course selfish but it is my desire that this money be useful to you. This talent of yours, of what does it dream? With what powerful themes has it not yet engaged? Ah, to be young and strong with the whole world before one! Think, search, open your mind and heart to what awaits you.

Good luck, dear friend,

Adelbert Delarue

PS. No, no, I must not apply pressure. Art is a mystery that in its own time happens as it will.

'Young and strong with the whole world before one'! Well of course he didn't know my age – it hadn't come up in our correspondence – but what made him think I was young and strong? My limewood gorilla was young and strong but he never would grow old and he had batteries to power his passions. At the moment I didn't have any passions.

I didn't like Delarue's letter. Although he said that he 'must not apply pressure', that's exactly what he was doing by attributing depths to my talent that simply weren't there. 'Powerful themes'! If I saw one coming towards me I'd cross to the other side of the road.

'Try to hold still,' said Mick Corbett. He paused every now and then to wipe away the blood and the excess ink. 'All right?' he said.

'Fine.'

He completed the outline, then changed to a rotary machine for the shading and filling-in. I suppose the whole thing took about half an hour, and when it was finished he applied surgical spirits to clean the tattoo, patted it dry, put on a small amount of antiseptic cream, then a dressing which I was told to keep on for one hour. There followed instruction for the care of my bat and a photocopied sheet headed TAT-TOO AFTERCARE. My bat cost forty pounds which was unquestionably a bargain if it could fly me to a better place.

'I hope it brings you luck,' said Mick Corbett as I left. I'd told him the bat was a happiness symbol. I looked at my watch to note the time so I'd remember when to remove the dressing, then I crossed the road, went down to the corner, and turned left into the North End Road. I was feeling receptive and half-expecting something significant to happen. After passing Blockbusters I crossed the road to the tiny plaza next to the church. There's a little raised garden with a couple of trees in it and a low retaining wall around it. This wall provides seating for a low-budget drinking community. Some of them look like pensioners, others are probably on the dole; I don't know whether the population changes but the numbers always seem about the same. Today there was a one-man splinter group who sat with his back against the church railings shouting something unintelligible in harsh monosyllables.

I walked past him and stopped outside the church, the Parish Church of St John, Walham Green. I'm in that part of the North End Road often but only now did I notice that the figure of Christ on the cross was not the one that used to be there. I remembered the old one as being made of wood and I remembered liking it. This new one was a fibreglass job as smooth as a surfboard and about the same colour as the dummy in my original Crash-Test toy. In face and form it was not unacceptably prettified but the high-gloss effect was perhaps a little slick for a redeemer. Jesus, I thought, you've come a long way since Tilman Riemenschneider.

The cross, a black one, seemed to be the old one, with the INRI scroll and the little roof over it. Towards the bottom of it was a brass plaque:

Originally erected
to the glory of God
and in memory
of members and past members
of the
17th Fulham and Chelsea Battalion
Church Lads' Brigade
who gave their lives in the war.

Restored 1997
in memory of
Lois Child
(1901–1996)
a faithful parishioner.

At the foot of the cross were flowers in vases and little candles, some of them overturned, surrounded by a circle of whitewashed bricks.

In my field of vision was a plane tree leaning over an illegible headstone. The tree and the headstone were dark in the foreground of the picture in my eyes; beyond them there was a sunlit vista of North End Road with people and traffic: a practical demonstration of life beyond the grave. Despite the sunshine it was beginning to rain. The light darkened, the sky became grey; a spotlight bracketed to the ground illuminated a corner of the church without shedding much light on Jesus.

I doubted that there was a Church Lads' Brigade in World War II; this memorial must have been erected after World War I. As the rain fell I imagined, helped by my recall of grainy newsreels, the Church Lads' Brigade with fixed bayonets going out of the trenches, over the top towards the enemy while Jesus in large and small crucifixes, in paintings and sculpture, in wood and in various metals, died for their sins. And now in fibreglass.

I went into the church where I found Father John Hunter, the curate, a tall, squarely built man in cassock and dog collar. Balding, with close-cropped grey hair and spectacles, he looked as if he was careful of souls and wary of eggs. The thirty-nine buttons on his cassock symbolised the Thirty-nine Articles of Religion and they were all buttoned up but I wondered if he ever found himself listening for something he couldn't hear.

I asked Father John about the old Jesus and he said it hadn't been wood but terracotta, shattered when the cross came down in a storm ten or more years ago and replaced a couple of years later by this one. The cross was the original one, restored.

Inside the doorway near the always-open chapel was a bulletin board to which were pinned an advertisement for Weight Watchers, handwritten notices from people looking for jobs and flats, and one that said CUT AND BLOW DRY. RING TONY.

7

SARAH VARLEY

Sometimes in the underground I close my eyes and the sound of the wheels on the rails and the surging and swaying of the carriage become the rolling passage of the years in the darkness of my mind: 1985 to 1993 rush towards me and away: my years with Giles.

He was a good-looking man, tall and blond, and his honest open face charmed everyone. He had strong hands, golden hairs on the backs of them in the lamplight. I used to feel safe in those hands but not quite safe enough to think of starting a family although Giles wanted to. He was good at starting things but so far hadn't gone the distance with anything and I was the only steady provider in our marriage. When he got into doll's houses I thought perhaps he'd found himself. He hadn't done anything like that before but he was good with his hands, good with tools; he already had a pretty well-equipped workshop but there were enough saws, gouges, drills and whatnot that he lacked to give him some happy hours at the ironmonger's.

He bought a book on the subject and built a beautiful nine-room Georgian house on a scale of one inch to one foot. He painted it but didn't furnish it. It took him four months which wasn't bad considering the work involved – the windows and doors alone took more hours than I'd have expected. We ate a lot of pistachios back then because he used the shells as cups for glue.

He put an ad with a photograph in *Homes and Antiques* and very quickly got a commission from a London collector to do a six-room Victorian house on the same scale as the Georgian one. 'The full size world's too much for me,' he said, 'but at one inch to one foot I might do quite well.' In six months he completed the Victorian house, painted and with electric lights but unfurnished, to the client's satisfaction, got a cheque for seventeen hundred pounds, and we drank champagne for the first time since loft extensions.

Commissions for a Queen Anne and a Regency followed the Victorian house, and the workshop became a place of ongoing action and contentment for Giles. When he came upstairs for meals he was often whistling, and he carried himself like a man who was putting meat on the table.

His next client was a woman in Bristol who rang him up and asked him if he could make her a copy of a seventeenth-century doll's house in the collection of the Rijksmuseum in Amsterdam. She was American and her name was Peggy Sue Wilson.

She sent Giles a museum booklet with detailed descriptions, illustrations, and measurements; it was obvious to me that this was a project that might take years. Giles of course was delighted at the prospect of conferences in Bristol and at least one trip to Amsterdam. This one was altogether a more serious undertaking than his last commission: the doll's house of Petronella Dunois, the daughter of a high official in The Hague, was a square oak cabinet veneered with walnut that stood two metres high on its barley-twist legs and displayed frontally the peat loft, the linen room, the nursery, the lying-in room, the salon or 'best room', the cellar, the kitchen, and the dining room. Every room was full of family and/or servants, furniture and every kind of artefact, all of which Giles intended to copy along with the complete decoration of the rooms. Even the veneering was nothing simple: it was walnut marquetry in a geometrical pattern of rosettes and stars. To me this looked like a job for an army of artists and craftsmen but Giles said he could do it. 'Don't forget,' he said with a crooked smile, 'this isn't the big world, it's the little one.'

'I hope you're getting paid in full-size money,' I said.

'Don't worry, I have a good feeling about this one but I can't do an estimate until we go to Amsterdam and I see what the job entails.'

So Giles and Peggy Sue went to Amsterdam. He took photographs, made sketches and notes, and came home rather pleased with himself. 'I'll get fifteen thousand for the house with nothing in it,' he said. 'That's not bad, is it? I'll do a separate estimate for the furnishings, the decorations, and the figures when I've finished the house.'

'What about your expenses so far – air fare, hotel, and the rest of it?' When he was feeling expansive he tended to brush details aside.

'I'll put the travel expenses on the invoice for the starting payment of five thousand pounds. I get five thousand more at the halfway point and the balance when the house is finished.' I could hear the pride in his voice; I was touched by it and happy for him but the size and complexity of the project made me anxious.

'You get the first five thousand before you start the work,' I said, 'right?' It was difficult for me to believe that someone called Peggy Sue was going to pay Giles any part of fifteen thousand pounds.

'Yes, I'm actually going to get five thousand pounds before I do anything. I am now on a par with roofers and builders and other guys who drive around in white vans with ladders on top.'

'When are you invoicing her?'

'As soon as I get proper business stationery.' So that was the first part of the job and it took two weeks and a couple of hundred pounds which resulted in reams of costly laid A4 headed *The Small World of Giles Varley*. A little twee, I thought. Maybe even unlucky.

The invoice did at length go out, the cheque came in; Giles went to Moss & Co in Hammersmith for the oak and walnut and got started. From then on he spent most of his time in his workshop. He intended to do the base with the barley-twist legs first; for this he needed complete accuracy in his calculations for the lathe work and he hadn't much time for conversation.

I went down there every now and then to see how it was going; I liked the smells of paint and glue remaining from the last doll's house and the smell of new wood from this one; I liked the work-bench with its vice and its jumble of tools and wood scraps and the green-shaded light bulb that made an island of warmth where he worked. Until now the basement had been a cosy place for me to visit but the atmosphere had changed and I could feel that this project was weighing heavily on Giles. 'There's a lot more to this one than there's been to the others you've done,' I said.

'You think it's too much for me?'

'No, I don't,' I lied. 'It's just that you don't seem to be having fun with it the way you did with the others.'

'Work can't always be fun – it's only a doll's house but we're talking museum quality here.' He had in his right hand a jointed folding rule, boxwood with brass hinges and pivot. It was marked in inches and centimetres; when the four parts of it were folded together it was nine inches long, and it opened out to a yard. The markings on it were clear and sharp; it was a device of exactitude, a reassuring thing to hold in the hand. He had been tapping his thigh with it as we talked.

It was obvious that he didn't want me watching him and I began to understand that he knew very well that he'd taken on too much; whether he'd done it to challenge himself or defeat himself I didn't know, but he wasn't the Giles I was used to and a distance grew between us.

The work seemed to require more meetings in Bristol than I'd have thought necessary and – inevitably, I suppose – I found a note in a pair of trousers I was taking to the cleaner's and there it was: fidelity was one more thing Giles had failed in. Love does not exclude arithmetic; I'd invested a lot of time and hard work in Giles and this was my return. Not good enough.

Giles swore that he'd got into Peggy Sue's knickers under duress, that he was afraid of losing the commission if he didn't let her have her way with him. His adultery had made me angry but his defence made me embarrassed for him, which was worse. What I resented most was the violation of my privacy: this woman had come into my life, she'd had the use of my husband, and although as far as I knew she hadn't been in the house I imagined her in our bedroom going through my underthings.

I relegated Giles to the guest room but I didn't ask him to leave; I hadn't ever defined a point at which it was no longer worthwhile to continue with him, so we continued. I carried on with the cooking and we had our meals together although with less conversation than before. It was a strange time for me because Giles's unfaithfulness bothered me less than the thought that he might not finish the doll's house with all its people and pots and pans and the rest of it. He kept out of my way as much as possible; when I was home I'd hear him down in the workshop and I wondered how the doll's house was coming along; he no longer talked about it.

Then the basement went quiet and he didn't turn up for dinner. I went down to the workshop to see what was what; he'd done the base of the cabinet with the barley-twist legs and he'd measured and cut the wood for the house and that was all. He left a note on the work-bench under his folding rule; all it said was:

Goodbye from the one-inch to one-foot man.

I stood there with the rule in my right hand, tapping the palm of my left. Nine inches; I opened it out to thirty-six inches and folded it up again.

The next thing was a call from Peggy Sue telling me that he was dead at her place in Bristol and there weren't going to be any more payments because he hadn't finished the job. That was seven years ago. I was more shocked than grief-stricken – not only had he left the job unfinished, he himself was unfinished and there was a great deal of work still to be done on him. Shortly after that, of course, the aloneness that had been growing inside me stepped out, stood in front of me, and said, 'Here I am.'

I see now that when Giles was alive I didn't really know what he was to me; now I do. The Yeats poem comes to mind with the lines about the mountain grass retaining the form where the mountain hare has lain; in the shape of Giles's absence I see what his presence was to me: there was love, there was romance, there was passion but the main thing about Giles was that he was like a house that has potential but needs a lot of work. That excited me at the beginning, less as time went on.

I was sorry he hadn't at least finished the doll's house. When I think about him now I wish I could have done better with him; I wish he could have done better with himself too. But I guess life is what you wish you'd done better with.

Still, for good or ill, life goes on. There's nothing to be done about the past; today is all there is to work with.

At Covent Garden things were middling along – as always I went around to see what was on offer before setting up but I made no brilliant acquisitions and nothing much happened when I was ready for customers. In the road between the Jubilee and Apple Markets the pigeons were routinely inspecting the cobbles in the presence of a sweeper and his cart. From Peter's snack bar came the aroma of frying bacon. The Punch-and-Judy man who performs between the tube station and the Apple Market probably hadn't set up yet; Punch and his wife and the baby, the crocodile and Jack Ketch and the Devil would be lying silent in their bag, waiting to erupt into violent life.

As the place filled up with tourists the buskers in the Apple Market were belting out the overture to *Carmen* which seemed to promise a lot of action but it wasn't happening where I was. As I made little adjustments to the display on my table I found myself, not for the first time, shaking my head over the business of buying and selling bits of other people's lives. All around me were objects clamorous with silent voices: grandfather clocks with pendulums grown dull;

rusted crampons; medals with faded ribbons; postcards of piers long since fallen into the sea; sightless stereopticons; dolls and toy soldiers owned by children now old or dead; and jewels no longer warm with the life of their wearers. Minute by minute the market was filling up with the gabble of voices and thronging of footsteps of people hungry for those morsels of other lives, eager to wake the silent voices of objects long unused and feel the touch of garments and jewellery long unworn.

The morning started out cool but quickly got hot and the heat seemed to make the punters haggle worse than usual; they'd pick up a necklace priced at fifteen pounds that had cost me ten, offer five, and be outraged when I held out for fifteen. Alison and Linda at the table next to mine were having the same kind of day.

I'd taken off my jacket and cardigan and was standing there in a sleeveless top when there appeared in front of me the man I'd seen at the V & A. 'You!' I said.

He was wearing a blue T-shirt and he pushed back the sleeve to show me the bat tattoo on his left shoulder. I felt a little flush of irritation when I saw it. 'Am I supposed to applaud?' I said.

'You've got one too,' he said, pointing to my exposed left shoulder.

'I've had this about seven years now,' I said. I suppose I needed to make the point that I wasn't nouveau tattoo.

He nodded acknowledgement of my seniority. 'Can I ask what made you do it?'

'You can ask.'

'Sorry.' He seemed about to say more, then decided not to.

I felt bad about discouraging him when he wanted to talk. 'What brings you here today?' I said.

'I come here every now and then – I'm always cruising for something that will turn out to be something I've been looking for without knowing it.'

'See anything here this time?'

'Not so far.'

'What do you do?' It seemed impolite not to show some minimal interest.

He looked away for a moment, then back at me, gave a little cough, and said, 'I'm a woodcarver.'

'Can you make a living doing that?' In the Jubilee Market we talk very openly about the facts of life.

'I designed a successful toy a while back and money kept coming in from that for a long time. Lately I've been doing private commissions.'

'I've never met a toy designer before. What kind of toy?'

'A crash-dummy in a radio-controlled crash-test car. The car springs back into shape after it's been crumpled and you can put it and the dummy back together and do the crash again.'

'What in the world gave you that idea?'

'My father was in the crash-dummy business.' He was examining a silver bangle in the shape of a snake. 'You have nice things here. Have you been doing this long?'

'Fourteen years.' As I said that a gypsy-looking woman picked up a garnet necklace, fixed me with a hard stare, and said very aggressively, 'How much?'

'Fifteen,' I said.

She expelled her breath scornfully and shook her head. 'Best price?'

'Fifteen.' I didn't like her manner.

I noticed then that my new acquaintance was holding the arm of a small dark man who looked as if he might be the woman's partner. 'He was walking away with this,' he said, holding up an opal ring ticketed at fifty pounds.

'You're crazy,' said the man. 'I just had it in my hand while I was looking at something at the other end of the table.' He tried unsuccessfully to pull away.

Suzy from two tables down the line came over for a look. 'These two were at my table last week,' she said, 'and after they left I was missing a brooch. Did you catch them in the act?'

'Not proveably,' I said. 'Let him go,' I said to my vigilant friend. 'It's your word against his and I've still got the ring.' To the woman and the man I said, 'I'd rather not see the two of you again and I'll pass the word to my colleagues.'

'Pfft,' said the woman. 'You got nothing we want.' She gave me a finger and strode off with her consort.

'Thanks,' I said to my security man of the moment. 'I always expect a certain amount of thievery but I'm glad not to lose that ring. I'm Sarah Varley, by the way.'

'Roswell Clark,' he said, and as we shook hands he noticed that my eyebrows had lifted at his name. 'I'm a little strange,' he said, 'but I'm not actually an alien life form.'

'Anyone in the family in the UFO business?'

'No.' He seemed a little embarrassed, and began to whistle a tune very quietly, almost under his breath, as he looked at the things on my table. Giles suddenly came to mind; he used to whistle in that introspective kind of way as he worked on his first dolls' houses. Even the tune seemed familiar. Was it one that Giles had whistled? Yes, because I was able to anticipate where it was going next.

'What's that you're whistling?' I said to Roswell Clark.

'"Is That All There Is?",' he responded with a half-smile.

'Well,' I said, 'I have no further questions at this time.'

'That's the title of the song.'

'Oh. Do you know the words?'

'"Is that all there is?"' he sang very quietly. '"Is that all there is?/If that's all there is, my friends,/Then let's keep dancing,/Let's break out the booze and have a ball/If that's all there is."'

'Is that all there is?' I said. 'To the song, I mean.'

'That's just the refrain but it pretty well says it all. The recording I have is by Peggy Lee. In the song she tells in successive verses how her house burnt down, how her father took her to the circus, how she fell in love with a wonderful boy who went away and she thought she'd die but she didn't, and after each verse she asks, "Is that all there is?" to a fire or to a circus or to love. Then she sings, "I know what you must be saying to yourselves – If that's the way she feels about it, why doesn't she just end it all?" But she says no, she's not ready for that final disappointment because she knows that when she's breathing her last breath she'll be saying, "Is that all there is," and so on. Are you all right? You've gone pale all of a sudden.'

'Funny thing about songs,' I said, 'what they'll bring back.'

He was looking at me as if I'd blurted out my whole history with Giles. 'Do you think that's all there is?' he said.

I don't open up for strangers and not all that much for friends but he seemed so much in need of a straight answer that I said, 'Not until you're dead. As long as you're alive there's still a chance for more than there's been so far.'

His face brightened, he really had quite a nice smile.

'I'm glad you said that. Let me buy a coffee for you and your neighbours.'

'Thanks.' I introduced him to Alison and Linda. 'Small

black coffee for me, with sugar,' said Alison. 'Large milky tea with sugar for me,' said Linda. 'I'll have a white coffee, not much milk, no sugar,' I said.

As Roswell left, the buskers in the Apple Market were doing the *habanera* with a rather good contralto. Her voice rose above the hubbub of the market, drifted on the sunlight and the heat of the day.

Alison nodded approvingly in Roswell's direction. She's a tall stout woman with green butterfly spectacles and red hair that she wears short. She's fifty or so and looks like the cynical friend who's seen everything but she's not cynical at all. 'New friend?' she said.

'Acquaintance,' I said. 'I met him at the V & A.'

'I picked up my first husband at the V & A,' said Linda. She's a small woman closer to sixty than fifty, neat figure, close-cropped grey hair, does yoga, mostly wears black.

'But you put him down again,' said Alison.

'Nothing's for ever,' said Linda. 'It was OK for three years.'

Carmen was now into the *seguidilla*. I visualised her tied up and sitting in a chair in the Apple Market while Don José passed the hat. I too was tied up, by a very large woman who was almost as wide as my table and effectively blocked it from other punters. I'd seen her several times before this and she'd never bought anything. She's from Leeds and she collects Scottish terriers – figures, brooches, whatever. 'I've got two real ones,' she said, 'Glen and Fiddich. They're adorable. Do you have a dog?'

'I've got a Butler & Wilson French-poodle brooch here but no Scotties.'

'I mean a live dog, the kind you take for walks.'

'No, I don't.'

'My two are so clever – when they see me getting ready to go out they run and get their leads and wait for me by the door. They love to get into bed with me when I watch television. They especially like those old Lassie movies. Children might disappoint but dogs never.'

'Do you have any children?' I was trying to see around her for prospective customers but I wasn't having much luck.

'No,' she said, and at this point Roswell appeared with the coffee and tea and gently and apologetically overlapped into the space she was occupying so that she was eased out of it. 'Don't forget,' she said as she removed herself, 'I'm always in the market for Scotties!'

As we drank our coffee and tea there appeared one of my regulars, a pleasant and enthusiastic woman from New York who likes to spend money on costume jewellery. Florence, her name is, but I always think of her as Floradora because of her flamboyance. She's a small woman but dresses as if she were a large one, favouring large prints in bold colours and jewellery that can be seen clearly from a distance. Today her frock featured red cherries as big as oranges on a black background. She wore her grey hair in a beehive, with red-framed spectacles, red plastic hoops in her ears, and a necklace of shiny plastic cherries and green leaves. Florence is secure with her style; she knows what she likes, has fun looking for it, and enjoys being herself. I like her for that. Plus she puts her money where her taste is.

'What've you got for me?' she said. 'I haven't bought anything yet this trip, I've been saving myself for you.'

I took out the Schiaparelli necklace and earrings I'd been keeping under wraps with her in mind. Purply and iridescent, shimmery and splendid, they would have looked good on a six-foot showgirl. 'What do you think?' I said.

'Mmmm!' said Florence. 'You know me too well. I surrender. Will I leave here with enough money to get back to the hotel?'

'You're a regular,' I said, 'and I'll give you a friend's price which is a little better than I'd give a dealer.'

'I appreciate that. How much?'

'Three hundred.'

She blew out a little breath and nodded. 'Worth every penny too; there's not enough sparkle in the world.' She counted out six fifties, I wrapped the necklace and earrings in tissue paper, put them in a small Harrods bag, and we shook hands. 'Now I'll need a new dress,' she said. 'A woman's shopping is never done.'

'Life is hard. Be brave. Come back soon.' We were all smiling after Florence left. The money made this a good day but my main satisfaction came from having judged correctly that she'd go for the Schiaparelli. The buskers in the Apple Market had finished with *Carmen* some time ago and were waltzing with Johann Strauss, *Tales from the Vienna Woods*. All the aisles between tables were full of people by now, eyes hard with acquisitiveness, their mouths busy with buns and coffee, the money in their wallets and purses eager to jump into ours. The lilt of the music lifted the sounds and smells of the market, the voices and the footsteps and the pigeons plodding on the cobbles, and I hummed along with it.

Roswell had picked up a little Goebel china figure from my table, probably from the fifties, a model of a nutcracker, one of those toothy chaps with tremendous jaws worked by a lever in the back. He was four inches high with a bushy white beard, wearing the uniform of Frederick the Great's tall troopers: blue shako with a red plume, short red frogged jacket, white trousers with a blue stripe, shiny black boots.

He was holding his sword upright against his shoulder and grinning heroically with his many teeth. He wasn't a working model, couldn't crack nuts, and if enlarged to full human scale would be very short and stubby; but he seemed cheerfully capable of crunching any difficulty whatever. Not a failer.

Roswell was grinning back at the little china man. 'This one talks to me,' he said. It was priced at twenty and he reached for his wallet.

'Put away your money,' I said. 'You caught a thief, saved a ring, and brought me luck. Have it as a little thank-you from me.'

'He's a short guy but that's a big thank-you,' said Roswell. 'Thank *you*.' He seemed about to say more, blushed, decided not to, looked at his watch, said, 'I haven't done any work yet today. See you.' And left. Whistling 'Is That All There Is?'.

Alison and Linda were looking at me in a smirking sort of way.

'What?' I said.

'A famous madam,' said Linda, 'once said that when you start coming with the customers it's time to leave the business.'

'I'm not all that professional,' I said, 'and I'm feeling expansive. This is one of the good days.'

8

ADELBERT DELARUE

Strongly intriguing, is it not, the variety of ways in which we humans replicate ourselves? I do not speak of the process of reproduction here, no. I have in mind dolls, models, puppets, toys soft and hard, with clockwork and without. I have a little tin clockwork porter who pushes a tin trolley piled high with tin luggage. I have a smiling plastic gymnast who does marvellous things on the bar and never tires as long as his clockwork is rewound. I have a tin ice vendor who pedals his icebox tricycle but has no tin customers. These little toy people do the same as their human counterparts but they do not relieve the humans of their duties.

I think now of crash-dummies, little ones first. The wooden two who make love to the sound of a crash, their black-and-yellow discs emphasise the motion of their bodies. So erotic is the sight of them as with blank blind faces they couple without fatigue and inspire Victoria and me to new heights of passion. Why should the action of these dummies have that effect? I think it is because always more sexual excitation is needed, and to see the toy copulating while we do the same is exciting. And there move with us the black-and-yellow discs we have painted on ourselves. Other elements come into it; there was a film called *Crash* in which the Eros/Thanatos theme was explored with many crashes and sexual acts. It goes without saying that the meeting of hard metal and soft flesh is provocative, and to be naked in a car is already an acceptance of whatever may follow. But this is not what is now uppermost in my mind.

Car crashes arise from drunkenness and careless driving, excessive speed and sleeping at the wheel. These are sins for which many die each year. In the hope of avoiding death we strap dummies into cars and make them die for us. From these harmless deaths we gather data so that we may crash without dying.

Sometimes in the small hours of the night Victoria and I paint our bodies with black-and-yellow discs and our nakedness we cover with black silk dressing-gowns. Then I ring for my chauffeur Jean-Louis and he knows that I want the black Rolls-Royce with the black windows. In the car, quick, quick, we are again naked. Under us the leather upholstery is cool in summer, warm in winter. The Rolls-Royce hums smoothly through the quiet streets, then on to the Périphérique where it acquires speed. On either side rush past the darkness and the lights of Paris and as we fasten ourselves to each other I feel the black-and-yellow discs moving with us and I imagine the impact, the noise and the pain of a high-speed crash. Strange, is it not, what games the mind will play? The crash that impends always, the sudden violent death are built into this road and this motorcar that wants always to go faster. The death in the road and in the machine, the velocity of the car and the feel and smell of the upholstery excite us, cradle us as we give ourselves to each other and the night. We make love, then sleep and love again.

We sleep when Jean-Louis returns us to the Avenue Montaigne before dawn. He inserts a CD in the player and wakes us with Jan Garbarek's *Madar*. Another day begins; another night awaits us.

I am not an artist. In my house are works of art: Sèvres, Meissen, and Minton porcelain; glass by Gallé and Lalique; a Sevigny armoire; Hofmann chairs and tables and other pieces from the Wiener Werkstätte; Kelim rugs; a T'ang dynasty horse. On the walls are paintings by Daumier, Redon, Guardi, Whistler, and Waterhouse; drawings by Tiepolo, Claude, Friedrich, and Rethel. I can buy art and look at it and be moved by it but to produce it I have not the capability. I look at Daumier's little painting of Don Quixote and Sancho Panza and I try to feel how he felt when he painted it. I try to think his thoughts; I understand his use of light and shade and colour, the play of weights and volumes, the density of the tinted air in which Don Quixote on Rosinante and Sancho on Dapple are at the same time solid and ghostly, dream and reality. But if I were given a blank panel I could not see what he saw in it; my hand would not know what his hand knew when it held the brush. There is in my life nothing as good as what he did.

There will never again be a Daumier or a Claude; the time for that kind of seeing, that kind of thinking, is past. Art now is too often the childish showing-off of talentless poseurs supported by collectors at the cutting edge of idiocy. We are all of us strapped in a car that speeds towards a blank wall while crash-dummies race ahead of us to die for our sins.

What are the thoughts of Roswell Clark as I write this? In addition to the income from Crash Test he has now had from me seventy thousand pounds with which to buy unencumbered minutes, hours, days, and weeks. I have given him time in which to be open to what will come to him. What *will* come to him?

9

ROSWELL CLARK

OK. Deep breath. My wife, Jennifer. She taught flute at St Paul's School and she was a good-enough flautist to play with the London Sinfonietta. She was a handsome woman, tall and graceful, dark and brooding. She and I had a fair number of rows but we experienced the world together; if it looked like rain we both noticed it and said something about it; we read things out to each other from *The Times* and the *Guardian*, went to concerts and watched videos together. Now the world goes on without her; she's not here to see the nights and days, the rain, the changing of the seasons. At odd moments I want to tell her something or show her something, then it hits me again: she's gone.

It happened on a rainy Saturday night in November. We'd been to dinner with friends in Highgate. It was an OK evening; the *bonne femme* was good; the beef olives were good; the wine was good; the conversation was lively. We'd got around to talking about how busy everyone was, how most of us had more things to do than there was time for. 'Not Roswell,' said Jennifer. 'He has more time than things to do, but he keeps busy thinking about the things that nobody else has time for.'

'Einstein had the same problem,' I said.

'So when are you going to come up with a universal theory?' said Mark Simpson, our host.

'I'm working on a new relativity theory,' I said. 'This one is about wives and husbands.'

'That was more than Einstein could handle,' said Mark's wife Nicola, and then Toby Gresham got us into the subject of the expanding universe while Jennifer gave me a look that said, 'What?'

My answering look said, 'I really hate it when you explain me to people in that patronising way.'

'If what I said seemed patronising, that's *your* problem,' was her wordless reply. 'Expansion can be a bad idea,' said Jessica Gold. 'Look what happened when Biba moved into Derry & Toms,' and the conversation went on in various directions along with the cognac and the grappa.

'Don't forget that you're driving,' said Jennifer as my glass was refilled.

'How could I, with you to remind me?'

'More coffee?' said Nicola.

It was pouring when we left; the streets were very black and shiny; the headlights of oncoming cars lit up curtains of rain, the windscreen-wipers flopped back and forth like an endless argument and in our little room on wheels the atmosphere was getting thicker. I said, 'I really hate it when you explain me to people in that patronising way.'

'If what I said seemed patronising, that's *your* problem,' said Jennifer. 'Shouldn't you have taken a right back there?'

'Probably,' I said. We didn't visit the Simpsons that often, and on the return trip the one-way system in Camden Town sometimes defeated me. Things got blacker and more spaced out with dim lights here and there and I realised that we were in the usual wrong place somewhere around King's Cross.

'How much did you have to drink?' said Jennifer.

'Not enough,' I snarled as I swung the car around into an intersection that seemed very dark and undefined.

'Look out!' said Jennifer as we were hit on the passenger side. Her last words.

I haven't driven since.

10

SARAH VARLEY

'Stop it, Sarah,' I said to myself. Because I could feel myself juicing up to make this man do better. He was failing in some way, he was putting out failure pheromones and they were getting me excited. Not for sex but for the hardcore depravity of trying to build towers out of wet dishcloths. He was very evasive in conversation; what was he hiding? For that matter, what was *I* hiding by turning my critical faculties on him rather than on myself?

How had Giles and I fallen in love? I met him in 1984 when I was twenty-eight. Twenty-eight! Sometimes that seems a hundred years ago. My name was Burton then and I was working at the Nikolai Chevorski Gallery in Cork Street. Chevorski always reminded me of the joke about the man who packaged goatshit and sold it as brain food. I was on the gallery staff because he'd seen me there the year before and offered me a job on the spot. He was a short man and he liked to have tall women around him. At the time I was with a small firm of auctioneers who were about to go out of business so I was happy to make the move.

The show at which I was hired by Mr Chevorski was

entitled *Haruspications* and featured twenty-four large paintings of chicken guts by Winston Breck. Like most of the
shows at that gallery it received a good deal of attention.
Seymour Daly of *The Times* said, 'Although it might be
argued by some that Breck has chickened out, he has done
it in a gutsy manner, and by doing it in our collective face
he has forced us to see what we may have looked away from
before this.' Noah Thawle of the *Guardian* said, 'Semiotically
baleful in their revelation of what one would rather not see,
these paintings with their anatomical mysteries have a visceral
impact that augurs well for Breck's future.' Lucy Camaro of
the *Daily Telegraph* predicted that 'Breck's paintings may well
convert more than a few of his viewers to vegetarianism but
inviting one, as they do, to descry a personal destiny in the
mantic disembowelment of chickens, they exert a terrible
fascination.' Lena Waye of the *Independent* found '. . . the
metaphor less than inspired. It may be that those who pay
money for old rope will splash out on chicken guts; and
the art market being what it is, they can always sell them
at a profit.'

Before the show had even opened George Rubcek and
Darius Fitzimmons had bought three of the paintings for their
collection, so the word was out that the oracles had said yes.
'I don't really know much about this kind of brain food,' I
told Chevorski.

'All you need to know,' he said, 'is that George Rubcek
and Darius Fitzimmons have already bought three, so now
the herd punters will pay big money to have him on their
walls and they can dine out on it for two or three months.'

The evening a year later when I met Giles was the opening
of Cyndie Dubuque's show at the gallery. Giles arrived with
a woman of fifty or so who was in somewhat better shape

than she really was. She had dyed red hair with a frizzy perm and wore a blue leather jacket, white T-shirt, jeans that had been sprayed on, and brown cowboy boots. Giles was thirty at the time, not exactly a toy boy but I doubted that his connection with the enhanced mother-figure was altogether non-commercial. He was as ruggedly handsome as a film star and he looked at me the way a man who knows horses looks at a horse. I was a lot younger than I am now, which is to say that when I saw Giles I saw potential; I wasn't sure what kind but I was willing to have a go at developing it.

Cyndie Dubuque was an American painter who'd dedicated herself to the celebration of the clitoris. This was back before the Internet when the clitoris still had some novelty value and the opening was well attended. I saw Seymour Daly, Noah Thawle, Lucy Camaro, Lena Waye, Thurston Fort of the Royal Academy, and Folsom Bray of the Post-Modern Gallery, whose praise added zeros to any price. George Rubcek, with a face like a sticky bun with two raisin eyes, was there. He said that Darius would have come but he was laid up with the flu. Darius is dead by now of AIDS and Cyndie Dubuque hasn't been heard from for a long time but that evening was all go. The champagne wasn't vintage but many of the chequebooks were, and Cyndie got so carried away that she had to be restrained from dropping her knickers and exhibiting the most recognisable feature of her self-portraits.

The champagne and caviare were being handed round by sleek young women in white shirts, red bow ties, very short black skirts, spike heels and black stockings that ended in a flash of thigh and red suspenders. These girls were provided by the caterer, Fizzy Lizzy, and would be somewhere else tomorrow; I as permanent staff was in a little black dress that was almost as short as the pelmets of the Fizzy Lizzy cup-bearers but I wore tights instead of stockings and suspenders; this didn't discourage Nikolai Chevorski from groping my bottom but he was just over five feet tall so his world-view was closer to the ground than most people's.

While his frizzy-permed friend was talking to George Rubcek the as-yet-unmet Giles made his way through the minglers and networkers to me, his sexuality shimmering like a motorway mirage. 'You look too real for this kind of thing,' he said to me.

'That's because I'm getting paid for it. On my own time. I'm no realer than you are.' I was reading him the way you read the little film blurbs in the TV schedule: 'Predictable story attractively packaged but short on plausibility,' this one said. It's difficult for me to believe how cynical and naive I was at the same time back then. Not, however, cynical enough to avoid a man who needed improving.

I have a good collection of videotapes, among them favourites that I've watched several times by now: *Women on the Verge of a Nervous Breakdown*; *We Don't Want to Talk about It*; *The Red Squirrel*; *Junkmail*; *Near Dark*; *The Match Factory Girl*. In *Women on the Verge of a Nervous Breakdown* I identify with all of the women; in *We Don't Want to Talk about It* I feel so sad for Marcello Mastroianni who falls in love with and marries a dwarf who leaves him to join a travelling circus; in *The Red Squirrel* I'm convinced that Julio Medem used the idea of Ambrose Bierce's 'An Occurrence at Owl Creek Bridge', a tale of the American Civil War in which an apparent escape and return home are revealed to be happening only in the mind of a hanged man at the moment of death. I think the love story in *The Red Squirrel* is a posthumous one and I am haunted by the if-only of it. I love the unreliable postman in *Junkmail* who, having copied the keys left in a young woman's mailbox, is hiding in her flat when she attempts suicide. He pulls her naked and dripping from the bath in which she's overdosed and is about to drown and I'm so happy for them every time although God knows what they'll do with each other after he follows her offscreen at the end. In *Near Dark* I'm touched by the vulnerability of the vampire girl and delighted when her lover unvampires her with a transfusion of his healthy blood.

Of these films the one that stays with me most is *The Match Factory Girl*, written and directed by Aki Kaurismaki. The match factory is in Finland, Helsinki maybe. We see the logs that once were living trees being stripped naked; we see them reduced to sheets of matchwood, we see boxes of matches, each one the same as the others, on a moving belt as the machinery clanks out the minutes and hours. Day in and day out Iris (pronounced Earriss) checks the boxes of matches as they come off the production line. Kati Outinen is Iris; she's one of those unpretty actresses who can look beautiful or plain as required: in this film she looks plain. Iris lives with her middle-aged mother and the man who's moved in with her mother. She hands over her pay every week and cooks and cleans for them while they drink vodka (none for her). On the TV news a man stands in front of a line of tanks which come to a stop in Tiananmen Square.

Iris goes to a dancehall where she is the only woman not asked to dance. She sits alone by the wall while the ensemble plays a tango and the man at the microphone sings, with subtitles:

> Somewhere beyond the ocean
> there is a distant land

where warm waves softly caress
its ever-joyful sands.
Varieties of lovely flowers
bloom all the year around.
No cares, no worries there,
no troubles, and no gloom.
Oh, if I could only reach
that land of dreams some day,
then I would never, ever fly
from paradise away.

The singer wears a white suit, a burgundy shirt, a white tie. He's clean-shaven, has pomaded black hair. He's backed by a violin, guitar, accordion, and drums. Behind the musicians is a backdrop on which a few trees droop wistfully against a glaucous sky as the couples revolve to the music. That tango and the words of the song open the floodgates to a sadness that doesn't seem to be particularly mine; it's a universal sadness. A singer and four musicians and a tango with a green-sky backdrop in a place of ice and snow!

Next payday Iris doesn't give the whole pay envelope to her mother; she buys a red party dress, fixes herself up, and goes to a place with dancing and a bar where she's picked up by a man who takes her home, sleeps with her, leaves some money on the bedside table the next morning, and goes off to work. This man (his name is Aarne) wants nothing more to do with her and when she asks to see him again he takes her to dinner and tells her to go away.

Iris is pregnant from that one night and she hopes for a happy family life with Aarne. He tells her to get rid of the baby and gives her money. She steps in front of a car, is knocked down, and loses the baby. While she's in hospital her mother's partner comes to give her an orange and tell her to find somewhere else to live.

When she gets out of hospital her brother takes her in. She buys rat poison and goes to Aarne's flat where she says she won't bother him any more but wants to have a goodbye drink with him. She puts rat poison in his drink, then goes to a bar where another man makes an approach. She puts rat poison in his drink, goes home, is allowed in by her mother, lays the table, and puts rat poison in the vodka for her mother and her mother's boyfriend.

As she waits for them to die we hear the tango singer and his ensemble again and read the subtitles:

> Oh, how could you turn
> all my sweet dreams
> into idle fancies?

The song continues and we see Iris again at her job in the match factory as the police come for her. Having stopped the tanks, she goes with them quietly.

> When you give everything
> only to be disappointed
> the burden of memories
> gets too hard to bear.

Why have I got so many videos that I watch more than once – made-up people acting out made-up stories? The people and the stories aren't real but the ideas are: the ideas of true love and happiness, of lost love and sadness, life and death. We get such a little bit of time and it's so hard to find a life-story that works for us. Why have I given the story of *The Match Factory Girl* and taken up all this space to do it in? I'm not sure. Iris's story is nothing like mine but there's something about it that won't let go of me. Those tango songs!

11

ADELBERT DELARUE

Truly, it is not that I am simply a wealthy sybarite. (Are there poor sybarites?) No, to me there is more than that. I do not flaunt myself as a doer of good works but in that sphere I am not idle, not unknown. I have given thousands of millions of francs to all the major charities and some that are minor, even unknown. Why do I mention this? Life is a fast-flowing river of moments; to step into this river is to find it each time never the same. Last night I had a dream in which . . . No, I won't talk about it just now. Everyone has dreams.

All the same, every morning is different, is it not? I wake up with Victoria warm beside me smiling in her sleep; last night was good; life is good. Certainly the dead don't have much fun. It seems I am given to reflection today. I ponder long the Crash Test toy that aroused my interest in Roswell Clark.

I do not look back over what I have written here before this and I do not want to; I speak from the ever-changing moment. I think I have a few words said on the metaphor of this toy, the profundity of it. These thoughts remain with me. We forward go at speed; we are stopped, WHAM! You, I, the world. 'Even the sea dies,' said Lorca in his

Lament for Ignacio Sánchez Mejías long before anyone knew about pollution or global warming. Even the sea dies.

I have given to many of the Holocaust and Holocaust-Survivor charities. Naturally nothing goes away. This, I think, is the first law of the remembering animal: nothing goes away. Gottfried von Peng, my father, has gone away but not as far as Genghis Khan, for example. He died full of years and billions. *Death as a Friend* is the title of a drawing by Rethel in which Gevatter Tod in hooded garb and sporting the scallop shell of the Santiago pilgrim tolls the bell for the old man who in his church tower has come to the end of his journey. Death of course can afford to be friendly – no one comes with a scythe to cut off *his* life.

The dream: Victoria and I were naked in the Rolls-Royce; Jean-Louis was driving us around the Périphérique . . . No, I don't want to be telling this, it's bad luck.

I want something from Roswell Clark. What it is I do not know. Certainly I have with this money primed the pump. What will he make? Of himself. What will he of himself make?

12

ROSWELL CLARK

No word from Delarue since the letter in which he wanted to know what my talent was dreaming of, the letter in which he said he must not apply pressure. Pressure, of course, was exactly what I was now feeling. He'd been very generous in his three commissions and I'd taken his money; now he was expecting something of me. What? I felt it heavy on my back and clinging like a giant squid.

What was my patron doing now? Enjoying himself probably, without a care in the world as he waited for the mouse of me to bring forth some kind of mountain. My workroom is on the top floor of my house, with a north-facing skylight and large windows. The daylight in that room has a cool objectivity that is sometimes a little more than I can handle; a bad drawing looks worse in that light; a clumsy carving looks clumsier. My saws and my chisels and gouges, my rasps and rifflers hang in their proper places on the wall. If I were to die today they would still be there, saying, 'What has he accomplished with us? What did his work amount to?' Sometimes I feel as if the world is closed to me and I'm walking around and around it looking for a door.

There were scraps of lime in the bin where I keep leftover

bits. These neat blond pieces of wood had once been parts of trees with leaves that stirred in the wind. Trees are living things; they have souls, they have significances; Odin, hanging on his tree through days and nights, acquired wisdom; Absalom was caught in a tree by his hair and was killed; Christ was crucified on the tree of his cross. Walk into a wood and you can feel the trees listening.

This bat tattoo, that's a laugh. Did I think it was going to get me off the ground, make me fly? And now I feel as if the bat is expecting something from me along with Delarue.

I looked at the china nutcracker on my work-bench; *he* wouldn't let expectations get him down, he'd crunch them: chomp, chomp. Of course he has the jaws for it. I mostly have music going when I'm working and I thought it might help to get me started now. I went through my CDs and selected a compilation of Argentine tango bands, and when it reached Carlos Gardel doing '*El Carretero*' I began to feel a little more comfortable. I understood only a few of the words but I thought a *carretero* might be a man with a cart and a donkey. The song has an evening sound; I saw the carter making his way through dimly lit streets past low houses and I had the feeling of having already done a day's work. It was still morning, however, and I hadn't done anything at all, hadn't earned the evening feeling, so I stopped the music and went out. 'Take me somewhere,' I said to my feet, and they headed for the North End Road.

In a few minutes I found myself at the Church of St John, standing in front of the fibreglass Jesus and thinking about wood and Tilman Riemenschneider. He did crucifixions and lamentations, he did annunciations and assumptions and he was never extravagant with facial expressions; he only went so far and he let the wood do the rest: Mary's face when she receives the news of the Immaculate Conception and her face when she looks at the dead Christ, the face of Jesus living and dead and the faces of the mourning women – all of these listen with the ghosts of trees and now there is fibreglass. 'Surf's up,' I said.

'You talking to Jesus?' said a deep voice behind me.

I turned. It was a member of the low-budget drinking community. I'd seen him the last time I was at the church: a black man, tall and burly, wearing jeans and a red T-shirt and holding a can of John Smith. He had the face of the black policeman in one of those buddy movies where the partner is white. His manner was discursive rather than aggressive. 'Fibreglass is OK for surfboards,' I said, 'but Jesus deserves wood.'

He sipped his beer and thought about this for a while. I wondered where he stood on aesthetics.

'Did you come here to pray?' he said.

'No. Did you?'

'Prayers are for children.' He pointed to the brass plaque in memory of the Fulham and Chelsea Battalion of the Church Lads' Brigade. 'Were their prayers answered?'

'I doubt it.'

'So you're not praying. What do you want from Jesus?'

'Nothing as far as I know.'

'You wouldn't be standing here,' he said like a patient tutor, 'if you weren't looking for something from him.'

'I don't know. Messages, maybe.'

'"By the rivers of Babylon,"' he said, '"there we sat down, yea, we wept when we remembered Zion."'

'Is that a message?'

'It's a psalm, Number 137.'

'I know that. Do you remember Zion?'

'Doesn't everybody?'

My mother had said that Zion was where it was a whole lot better than now and it was where you never get back to. The smell of oil and metal, cigarette smoke and Jack Daniel's came back to me with the lamplight and shadows of my father's workshop. Whatever he handled, whether a hammer or saw or a piece of wood, he handled in a way that made you feel good. He showed me how to use a screwdriver and a hammer and I tried to hold them the way he did. With an empty cotton spool, what they call a reel here, a washer, a rubber band and a wooden match he made me a spool tractor that crept along the basement floor until it was stopped by the skirting board. 'I guess everybody does,' I said. 'There are all kinds of Zions.' Thinking, as I said that, that the Zion I remembered had been Babylon to my mother.

'There's a lot of Babylon around here,' he said, and went back to his colleagues. I made my way home slowly, seeing the spool tractor crash slowly into the skirting board.

13

SARAH VARLEY

Every month Burnside Auctioneers in Ealing send me a catalogue; I make a pot of Earl Grey and start circling the lot numbers that look promising. It's a three- or four-cup job to get through it and budget my fantasies, cosy reading all the way. The viewings are on Tuesdays, the auctions on Wednesdays and Thursdays.

Burnside is nothing grand like Sotheby's or Christie's; it's small and cramped and not comfortably laid out. The viewings are always a hurly-burly with people jostling one another and idly curious non-buyers taking up space and standing in front of things I want to see. Last Tuesday I found nothing terribly exciting in my price range. There was Lot 186, 'A GERMAN .800 ART NOUVEAU 13-PIECE FRUIT SET by P & S Bruckman, the handles decorated with figures from mythology, cased £120–£180'. I was willing to go to one-thirty-five on that. With commission I'd be paying one-sixty so I'd try to resell it at one-ninety and would take one-eighty if I had to. It was nothing that made my heart beat faster and obviously I wasn't going to get rich on it.

There were various other lots I was prepared to bid on,

mostly silver or silver plate which I'd been having some luck with. I'm always hoping for treasures that others have passed by and a cardboard box caught my eye: Lot 339 was 'A collection of treen'. No estimate. It was a jumble of unimpressive wooden artefacts: carvings of Krishna, Lakshmi, and Ganesha from the duty-free at Bombay, some boxes that might have been Tunbridge ware but weren't, a miniature shoe, and a higgledy-piggledy of other bits and pieces not likely to set the world on fire.

Among the bits and pieces, all the way at the bottom of the box, was a painted wooden hand pierced by a wooden spike that nailed it to a fragment of a cross. The hand had been broken off a little way up the wrist and the whole thing was, by my tape measure, three and seven-eighths inches long. The painted blood was almost worn away as was the flesh colour. Shocking, that hand – the authority of it. It was a right hand; the index and middle fingers were curved reflexively around the spike in an effort to support the weight of the sagging body. Death by crucifixion, I remembered having read, was caused by the collapse of the diaphragm, and all of that pain and sorrow were in those two fingers. The carving was remarkable in the delicacy of its realistic detail, the beauty of the fingers and fingernails and wounded palm and veins of the wrist of that man whose symbolic blood was still drunk by his worshippers.

I know some hallmarks and some of the provenances of the things I buy and sell but I have vast areas of ignorance and this was from one of those. It was obviously very old, but although it probably came from something valuable it wouldn't be worth much as a fragment. I wasn't thinking of resale; I wanted it because it had spoken to me and couldn't be ignored. I put it back in the bottom of the box and covered it with the higgledy-piggledy as well as I could, hoping to make Lot 339 as uninteresting as possible.

The next day at the auction I got the German art nouveau fruit set for one-thirty-five and I did all right with my other selections but although this is something I do for a living I was in a completely non-commercial state of arousal when Max Burgess, the auctioneer, called out, 'Lot three thirty-nine, a collection of treen, possibly treasures for the discerning.' Max is a gingery man, large and broad; he was a Petticoat Lane barrow boy before becoming an auctioneer and his style has nothing of the introvert. 'Do I hear thirty-five?' he enquired. 'You don't want to pass this by and later think: If only!'

Nobody responded. I've learned to avoid early foot and I kept my hand down. I saw Stephen Faulkes there, a spiteful little man who loves to bid things up and always knows when to jump off and leave me to pay over the odds. It was a grey day, threatening rain, and I'm prone to acts of desperation on grey days.

'All right,' said Max. 'It's that kind of day – caution is uppermost. Will someone say twenty-five and help me to move on?'

Faces of stone met this heartfelt request.

'I have no shame,' said Max. 'My mind isn't strong. I feel rejected. Is there a kind soul here to say ten pounds?'

Stephen Faulkes's hand went up.

'Ship ahoy!' cried Max. 'Rescue is at hand! Where ten appears surely twelve cannot be far behind?'

Myra Kaufmann went to twelve. By two-pound increments Max got us up to thirty-seven. True to form, Stephen took us to forty and I upped it to forty-five and got Lot 339, breathing hard. I would have gone higher; when I stop feeling that way about things I'll know I'm dead.

14

ADELBERT DELARUE

I have no wish to push myself forward in these pages. I have been invited to set down some of my thoughts so I do it as well as I can. Today I am thinking of two visits I have made to Autun, an old walled town in Burgundy founded by the Romans.

In my head – is this not so with everyone? – there live images of scenes I remember, places I have been, objects of significance. Sometimes one of these images pulls me back to the time of its first appearance; then there comes to me the place, the scene with its reality heightened, its colour and detail by the force of memory made vivid.

One such image is that of the figure of Christ on the tympanum of the west portal of the Cathedral of St Lazare at Autun. In the eleventh century St Lazare was the patron of lepers; the tomb at Autun was said to contain all or at least part of him, so for the lepers it was a place of pilgrimage. For me too it is such a place although no part of me has yet visibly rotted away.

That the unclean might worship apart from the clean, the bishop and chapter of Saint-Nazaire caused a new church to be built for the lepers at Autun. It is in this church, the

Cathedral of St Lazare, that Gislebertus, that genius of the Romanesque, with chisel and mallet wrought his marvels from 1125 to 1135.

The first time I went there I was not alone. I was young and my companion was a beautiful girl called Solange Tessier. She was studying art at the Sorbonne and she wished to see what Gislebertus had done at St Lazare.

Solange's interest was purely artistic; she was Jewish but did not practise that religion. 'It takes no practice to be a Jew,' she said. 'Either you are or you aren't; two sets of dishes mean nothing.' Myself, I had been educated by Jesuits under the governance of a Father Toussaint. He laid great stress on obedience and enforced it with a flexible black paddle on the hands: the sinner was permitted to choose the time of punishment within a twenty-four-hour span. This method of instruction naturally encouraged atheism in those pupils who were that way leaning. Between God and me the divergence widened until I wholly rejected the deity served by Father Toussaint and his black paddle. So the carvings of Gislebertus at St Lazare, however profoundly pious, would be for me nothing more than pictures in stone.

At that time I had not yet come into my inheritance. I was on a student allowance, Solange also; therefore we travelled by train and bus. It was a Saturday evening in October, already dark when we arrived. We registered at the Hôtel de la Tête Noir in the rue de l'Arquebuse. Our key for Room 309 was on a ring attached to a miniature wine bottle with the name of the hotel on the label. Such key-rings were sold as souvenirs at the reception desk; I have one before me as I write this. I cannot say it is empty because it has no inside to be filled – it is only a solid piece of wood in the shape of a bottle.

A middle-aged German couple came in as we stood at the reception desk. The man spoke French with an accent that pushed the words ahead of him like hostages. He explained that he and his wife were touring Burgundy and enjoying the food and the wines. I pitied them that they were not us.

We bought a half-bottle of the local Chardonnay and one of the Pinot Noir and took them up to our room. It was a pleasant little room; the flowered bedspread and the cosy lamps welcomed us; the slanting ceiling embraced us as we embraced each other. The wine was round and juicy; we drank it by the window from where we viewed the Champ de Mars and the Mairie, illuminated and as full of detail as buildings in a model railway. Then we went out to see the cathedral for the first time.

Past dim cafés and ancient houses we walked uphill on narrow pavements. Many of the houses were dark and seemed empty; the streets were very quiet, with sometimes the sound and lights of cars, sometimes the single white eye and whine of a moped. Up the rue aux Cordiers we went, the Grande and Petite rues Chauchien and the rue des Bancs where we continued past the Musée Rolin to the Place du Terreau. There we saw the cathedral with its spire black against the dark sky.

Now there is a restaurant, Le Petit Rolin, just opposite the steps at the west portal of the cathedral. It was not there when Solange and I came to Autun; there were no sounds of diners and drinkers to distract us as we stood at the base of the steps and looked up at the tympanum. Spotlights pushed away the darkness from it and showed us the stone with a hard brightness not seen in the evenings of the twelfth century. This tympanum is a half-circle over the two great doors, the lintel supported by capitals at each end and a trumeau in the centre. The trumeau, with the figures of Lazarus, Mary, and Martha, is a reconstruction, the original one having been thrown away.

On the tympanum Christ, in high relief, presides over the Last Judgement. He is shown in an elliptical enclosure called a mandorla. His pose is fully frontal; his elbows are at his sides, his forearms extended, palms upturned; his knees are bent, his legs turned out. His face looks straight ahead; his mouth is slightly open; he seems without anger, seems entranced. He has become not so much a judge as a medium: through him like lightning pass divine mercy or implacable wrath. I was a hardened atheist, yes, but I cowered before this Christ, this living stone, when I saw him that first time. On the mandorla are carved the words: OMNIA DISPONO SOLUS MERITOSQUE CORONO QUOS SCELUS EXERCET ME JUDICE POENA COERCET [I alone dispose of all things and crown the just. Those who follow crime I judge and punish.]

'The one who was the victim is now the judge,' said Solange.

'He is the Lamb who was slain,' I murmured as if Father Toussaint stood over me. Forgotten verses from Revelation came to me: '"And the kings of the earth, and the great men, and the rich men, and the chief captains and the mighty men, and every bondman, and every free man, hid themselves in the dens and in the rocks of the mountains. And said to the mountains and rocks, 'Fall on us and hide us from the face of him that sitteth on the throne, and from the wrath of the Lamb: For the great day of his wrath is come, and who shall be able to stand?"'

Solange was watching me. 'Are you OK?' she said. 'It goes?'

'Yes,' I said. 'It goes.'

'"*Gislebertus hoc fecit.*"' She read the words carved in the stone at the feet of Christ. [Gislebertus made this.] 'It was done by a man, a stonecarver who was paid for the job. He did not descend the mountain with the tympanum under his arm.'

'I know,' I said. 'And in any case there is no God.'

'Adelbert, you piss into the wind.'

'What do you mean?'

'The belief in God *is* God. The God in people's heads does all the things God is meant to do, so He exists even for those who claim that He does not exist.' She spoke the word 'He' with a capital letter. 'And this God in the head of Gislebertus used him to carve this tympanum for the glorification of His only son.'

'I'm not sure I follow your reasoning.'

'That's OK.' She kissed me. 'God will forgive you.'

'So you believe in Him then?'

'How could I not? I prayed for an Adelbert kind of guy and He gave me you.' More kisses.

Filling the stone half-circle around Christ are angels with trumpets, the Holy Virgin, the saints, the weighing of heavenbound souls by the Archangel Michael and those of the damned by a hideous devil who opposes him. Below them on the lintel are the saved in ecstasy and the sinners in despair.

Those figures! Gislebertus, having called them into being, allotted them spaces in which to fit themselves and their actions. Their bodies and limbs grew long or short in such shapes as were necessary for their gestures. Motionless in the stone they walk, creep, sing, weep, crouch, leap; they have no rest from the life hammered into them by this stonecarver who chiselled his name under the feet of Christ. One particular sinner on the lintel caught our eye; his scream echoes in the silent stone as two great hands (nothing more is visible) grab him by the head to pull him up out of sight. 'Gislebertus could not refrain from showing us this,' said Solange. 'He was compelled.'

She had brought her Nikon with her; she was rarely without it; in our Paris walks she photographed every thing from every angle with short lenses and long ones, film both fast and slow. Now she put the camera to her eye and looked through the viewfinder. Then she slung the Nikon from her shoulder again without taking any pictures.

'No pictures?' I said. 'Even without flash you have enough light.'

She said, 'When we're home I don't want to look at a little glossy print of what the camera saw, I want the whole thing big in my eye as it is now. I owe Christ and Gislebertus that much.'

'Christ has got into your head?'

'He was a man. They hung him on a cross with nails through his hands and feet and gave him vinegar to drink. The nails tore his hands as his body sagged until his diaphragm collapsed and he could no longer breathe. Now at communion the believers eat his body and drink his blood. Here in stone he offers himself.'

For a while we were silent, then Solange said, 'This Gislebertus, I think he would have been a chain smoker if there had been cigarettes in the twelfth century. He was addicted to stone, I know that – he could not leave it alone. Every time he found an empty space of stone he had to let in Heaven and Hell. He was like Thelonious Monk with a chisel and mallet.'

'Thelonious Monk!'

'Exactly,' she said. 'Very funky and off-straight. The performances of Gislebertus had of course to be planned but they are like jazz improvisations in stone. I think he must have been an obsessive, and to such people the Romanesque style comes naturally: again and again they reiterate the folds in garments – you can almost hear the left hand doing the bass part while the right hand carves the tune.' Ah, Solange! She had a husky voice, her breath was sweet, her cheek cool in the fresh October breeze. She liked the sound of what she had said and gave me a sidelong glance and a little smile.

We went back down the rue des Bancs to Le Relais des Hautes Quartiers. There we drank Pinot Noir with our boeuf bourgignon and felt well pleased with the world. The quiet voices of the other diners and the clink of cutlery made a soothing background; the music was old standards, not too loud. By the light of the candle on our table we held with our eyes each other's faces. Then we walked slowly down to the hotel, went to our room and made love. As we lay in each other's arms afterwards Solange said, 'God is an idea I can understand but the Jesus thing baffles me.'

'How is that?'

'He is the redeemer, yes?'

'Yes.'

'He died for our sins?'

'Yes.'

'So now we sinners have a clean slate and we don't need a Last Judgement, do we?'

'That isn't how it works, Solange. Christ was the ransom for the many but one still needs to claim the benefit of what he did. If you believe that kind of thing, that is.'

'What is that benefit?'

'The restoration of your relationship with God.'

'Why does it need to be restored?'

'Because of the Fall, because of the Original Sin.'

'That's going back a long way!'

'That's why it's called the Original.'

'How does one claim that benefit, how does one get restored?'

'By having faith in Christ.'

'And that puts you right with God?'

'If you seek his forgiveness.'

'OK, so you have faith in Christ and you ask forgiveness from God, then you die. Then do you still have to go through the Last Judgement?'

'Yes.'

'What then, you get preferential treatment because you had faith in Christ and forgiveness from God?'

'It isn't that kind of thing. I was taught that if you have faith in Christ then he takes on himself the burden of your sins and enables you to restore your relationship with God. He does this out of love. "For now we see through a glass darkly; but then face to face: now I know in part; but then shall I know even as also I am known. And now abideth faith, hope, charity, these three; but the greatest of these is charity."' As I said those words I believed that it was possible to know and be known fully. I drew Solange closer to me, her long warm body. She was snoring gently. Charity is *caritas* in Latin, which expresses better what I felt for Solange.

The next day was Sunday. After a late breakfast at the hotel we checked out and walked around the town. In the Champ de Mars when it was time for lunch we had omelettes and a bottle of Pinot Noir at a bistro patronised by young locals with children and elderly ones with small dogs.

From there we once more ascended the hill to the rue des Bancs and the Musée Rolin where Gislebertus's Eve was to be seen. We paid at the reception desk and were directed to the room where Eve resided. A Japanese woman sat on a bench viewing her. By the door a man who looked like someone's nephew kept an eye on us. Eve and her bit of stone garden were in two pieces carefully fitted together. She was fixed to the wall against a background of black cloth. She would have looked quite different as part of the cathedral; here her isolation and the lighting put her as it were on centre stage.

'Well,' said Solange, 'here she is: the Original Sinner who gave Adam the fruit of the Tree of Knowledge.'

'Somebody had to get the ball rolling.'

'This is the first medieval nude. She used to be on the lintel over the north door of the cathedral but she was taken down and used as a building block in a private house when they mortared over the tympanum.'

'Who and why?'

'The cathedral chapter. In the eighteenth century the canons found Gislebertus not to their taste, so they covered up the tympanum and removed some of the other carvings. How do you like Eve?'

Eve was designed for a lintel and so is a horizontal composition. Her nudity is sinuous as she glides serpent-like through the foliage and grasses of the garden. Her face is contemplative; almost her mind might be on other things, possibly she hums a little tune as she reaches behind her for the stone fruit of the Tree of Knowledge. Does she think of what will follow from the eating of that apple?

'She is what she is,' I said. 'She is the mother of us all, a mystery.'

'I want pictures of her,' said Solange. 'This is a woman thing.'

As she brought her camera up to her eye the man seated near the door explained, with an apologetic expression, that there was an eight-franc charge for photography. I paid him and Solange photographed Eve from several angles, including a close-up of her bottom seen from the rear. 'She's only a relief really,' she said. 'I'd like to see what he'd have done with her in the round.'

While I pondered the Original Sin and later ones we went again to the cathedral where we looked at the tympanum in the daylight. The stone was grey, weathered and pitted; to my eyes it showed itself doubly: then and now, with Christ as always offering himself. The tympanum in my eyes went from something to nothing and back again; my mind could not contain it as one or the other.

We went into the cathedral and tilted our heads back to view the many Gislebertus capitals which had been spared by the canons. These were Bible stories in stone, from Noah's Ark to the fall of Simon Magus; also lesser-known scenes with grimacing devils and various fanciful creatures. I had little response left for these − my mind was filled with the Christ of the tympanum and the mystery of Eve.

We left the cathedral a few minutes before Sunday services began. The sky was clear, the sun was bright, and as we started back down the hill the bells of St Lazare suddenly pealed. 'There is a God!' they shouted with their great metal throats. 'Believe us!'

I turned back towards the cathedral as if pulled by a chain. 'They get paid to say that,' said Solange. 'It's their job.'

We had only our rucksacks with us so there was no need to go back to the hotel. We walked to the train station from where the bus for Le Creusot would depart. At the Hôtel de France bar opposite we had coffee and Poire William, then I wanted to take a picture of Solange. 'Better not,' she said, 'it's bad luck.'

'How is it bad luck?'

'Years from now the photograph will be with you but maybe I won't.'

'Where will you be, Solange?'

'I don't know. Gone, maybe.'

I took the photograph. I have it still but Solange is not with me. We loved each other; I thought we would be together always. On our return to Paris I departed for Dortmund for my annual visit to my uncle Dietrich von Peng, the executor of the estate. Solange also was leaving Paris for a two-week holiday in New York. She met a painter there and married him and now she lives in America. I had a letter from her: 'Dear Adelbert,' she wrote:

> What if you had not taken that photo? Remember the two great hands that grab the poor sinner by the head? Goneness is like that, always waiting to grab someone. Maybe the one being grabbed is not even a sinner; maybe Goneness reaches blindly for anyone, good or bad.
>
>   I remember all there was.
>
>   Solange

Nineteen Octobers passed, and in the twentieth I wished to see the Christ of Saint Lazare again. I desired also to hear the bells. I went without Victoria, without Jean-Louis and the Rolls-Royce. I went alone as a pilgrim. Taking only a rucksack, I walked from my house in the Avenue Montaigne to Franklin D. Roosevelt, where I took the RER to the Gare de Lyon.

There in the daytime it was like a labyrinth of the night. There were many large young people with backpacks as big as steamer trunks and many old people with trolley bags. I already had my ticket and seat reservation, so I went to Platform 13 where I found the 12.34 to Marseille and Saint-Charles. This train would stop at Chagny, from where a bus would take me to Autun just as it had taken the two of us long ago.

I boarded the second-class coach and went to my seat. Soon an old lady was ushered in by a young man who kissed her and left. The old lady smiled and sat down opposite me. She settled back with closed eyes for a moment, then took a computer game out of her handbag and began to play. Only one other passenger came into the compartment, a very abled-looking young man, powerfully built. He took a DISABLED seat by the window and peeled an orange.

I closed my eyes and gave myself to the journey. I had no wish to relive old times; I wanted to stay in the present October to receive what new thoughts might come to me.

I opened my travel book: *Riders of the Purple Sage*, by Zane Grey, an English edition. Closing my eyes again I saw the rustlers' cavern behind the waterfall and I saw Bern Venters shoot the Masked Rider, who turned out to be a beautiful girl. He tended her wound and took her to his hidden valley. "'I'll try – to live,' she said. The broken whisper just reached his ears. "Do what – you want – with me."'

The train was moving. We glided under gantries and wires, past coloured lights and signals of various kinds. Through zones of bleakness we passed, then through human habitations. Sometimes files of poplars marched rearward beyond the gantries and the wires while TGV trains shot by us like thunderbolts. Strange towers and stretches of flatness appeared and disappeared; haggard landscapes, rivers and canals. Graffiti on walls, bridges, and power stations offered illegible messages, some perhaps for me.

Were there so many electrical towers nineteen years ago? Birches, poplars, and willows tried to remember Claude as they struck wistful poses: 'Was it like this?' they said. 'Was it like that?' The paper sign on the outside of the window said MARSEILLE backwards over sky, trees, hills, valleys, farms, rivers, boats and bridges. At Sens there were little trees on the platform with straight trunks and round leafy tops that might have been done by the Douanier Rousseau.

As we travelled on I found myself looking within more than without. Père Lachaise Cemetery appeared on the screen of my memory in the October of four years ago with the yellow leaves of autumn scattered among the tombs. Women sort themselves according to the famous dead they visit; I recall a lady I met at the tomb of Seurat: she was dotty but nice. And of course always at the supine statue of Victor Noir there are those who rub themselves against him and easily transfer their attentions from a bronze member to a live one. The dead are never lonely in Père Lachaise and the living need not be.

At the time I speak of I was without a long-term female friend, and being a romantic I craved the company of a like-minded person. I went to where Chopin lies, a little south of Bellini and east of Cherubini, near the Carrefour du Grand Rond. The paving stones glistened from the soft rain that had fallen a little while ago; the sky was grey and gentle, the trees sympathetic; almost I could hear a shadowy mazurka as I approached.

I stopped about three metres from the tomb to watch a young woman who was standing before it. She was looking at the marble muse who sits grieving for the departed composer. At the muse's feet were fresh flowers. Below her, in an oval inset on the plinth, is a relief profile of Chopin.

The woman was wearing jeans, black boots, a yellow wind-breaker, and a black baseball cap with the insignia of the New York Yankees. She had a large shoulder bag. She was short and plump, with a round face and short straight blonde hair. She shook her head sadly and put her bag on the ground, then she took a half-bottle of champagne and two glasses out of it. I was not close enough to read the label on the champagne. She popped the cork which flew straight up, then fell at my feet; she filled the glasses. She raised one to the marble muse, then poured it over the flowers. The second glass she raised to Chopin's profile, then drank.

Again she shook her head, took a paper bag out of the shoulder bag, put the two glasses in it, placed the bag on the ground and stamped on it. I moved towards her. 'End of a romance?' I said.

She turned to me with tears running down her face. I held out my arms and she moved into them. That was how I met Victoria Fawles. The champagne was Pol Roger; I have kept the bottle.

The next stop was Laroche–Migennes; after that came Tonnerre. Sometimes the window filled up with sky, leaving only a thin residue of earth at the bottom of the glass as we continued in a southeasterly direction. Montbard came next. The old woman and the young man had left the train at Tonnerre and there were other people in the compartment now but my mind and my vision did not focus on them. Superimposed on the wall opposite me was the mental image of the tympanum of the west portal of St Lazare. Although Christ is the judge he seems to be pinned there like a butterfly with outspread wings. If there were a God, might He have punished His only son in this way? Might He have said to Christ, 'You and your big ideas! You took it on yourself to be a ransom for the many; now the many are your problem, and you can judge them through all eternity.' What a thought.

Sometimes there were hills. It became sunny and we were at Dijon. Here the train stood for a long time while backpackers drank mineral water and Coke and bought things at the vending machine while their shadows did the same. Does Solange remember when we shared an orange at Dijon? I licked the juice that ran down her chin.

South of Dijon we passed vineyards. Next came Beaune, then Chagny, a peaceful little station where I and several others left the train for the 16.43 bus for Autun. Our driver was a short sturdy woman who conversed non-stop with a friend in the first seat while smoothly passing oncoming traffic in streets only wide enough for one car. Then up and down on winding roads through vineyards we went, through Nolay, Epinac, Sully and many smaller towns and villages to arrive at Autun at 18.06.

Through the October darkness I walked slowly up the hill to the Hôtel de la Tête Noir, putting my feet into the footsteps of nineteen years before. Almost I expected to smell the fragrance of Solange's hair if I turned my head. I registered at the hotel and was given, as I had requested, the key to Room 309, attached by a ring to its miniature bottle. I bought a half-bottle of Pinot Noir, then went up to the room where Solange and I had lain in each other's arms, had slept and awakened together. I had told myself that I was not going to relive the past but of course this is not possible: what we call the present is only the accumulated past.

I went to the window and raised my glass to the lights of the Champ de Mars and the Mairie. When I had finished the wine I went out and walked to St Lazare past the same dim cafés and ancient houses as before while cars and mopeds passed me going up the hill. At the cathedral I stood with my back to Le Petit Rolin and looked up at the tympanum that Solange and I had looked at together. 'Speak to me,' I said to Christ. 'Speak to me as the son of God. Tell me something.'

'I have nothing to say,' said Christ. 'This is all there is.'

'But meaning,' I said, 'there must be meaning.'

'Reality has no meaning,' said Christ, 'it is only itself. I am only myself; I am an image carved in stone. *Gislebertus hoc fecit.*'

'That is not a good enough answer,' I said. 'You're being evasive. Ideas are part of reality. There came to me the idea to travel here to see you and it meant something to me.'

'What?' said Christ.

'I don't know. That's what I'm asking you.'

'I don't know what this idea meant; sometimes people say they've come to see me when they really want to see someone or something else. Maybe God knows.'

'Are you saying there is a God?'

No answer.

I begin to be tired of talking about this. The next day I looked at the tympanum by daylight and still Christ said nothing. As I turned to start down the hill the bells shouted, 'There is a God! Believe us!' I waved goodbye without turning around, and walked down to the Hôtel de France where I had coffee and Poire William. Then I took the bus to Le Creusot where I got the TGV train to the Gare de Lyon; from there the RER to Franklin D. Roosevelt, and from there I walked home. No longer was I looking for meaning but still I wanted something and I had no idea what it might be.

15

ROSWELL CLARK

Last night I dreamt that Jennifer and I were with some kind of tour group; I don't know where we'd come from or where we were going. We'd had to move out of one hotel into another and we were worried about flight connections. A bellhop in a red jacket with brass buttons said, 'Would you like to upgrade your menu?' and gave us two very large shiny menus with illustrations in colour. We couldn't make out what the pictures were and there were only a few words in English, randomly jumbled together with several other languages. It was a sickening sort of dream, and when I woke up out of it I fell back into it.

It's true that I'm not sure where I'm coming from and I don't know where I'm going. I've had to move out of what was before and I don't know how to make the connection to whatever's coming next; I've no idea what's on the menu although I'd like something better than what I've had on my plate since Jennifer's death.

About six months after the crash I went to see a Dr Wakem. He was Martin Gold's therapist and Martin swore by him. 'A no-bullshit kind of guy' was how he described him.

'Depression,' said Dr Wakem to me, 'is anger turned against the self.'

'It's more than anger,' I said. 'I hate myself.'

Dr Wakem was a stocky man with close-cropped sandy hair and a bullet head that looked as if he could knock down walls with it. His blue eyes also seemed very hard. He fixed me with a cold stare, then lowered his bullet head as if he might butt me through the wall behind me. 'Why do you hate yourself?' he said.

'I killed my wife by drinking too much and driving without due care. That reason enough?'

'Definitely.' He nodded in a satisfied way, like the man who comes down the ladder to tell you that you need a whole new roof. 'How long ago was this?'

'A little over six months.'

'What actually happened?'

'Another car hit us on the passenger side. It was at night, raining, very dark. I never saw that car until it hit us. The driver just backed up and took off, I didn't get his number. Or hers, if it was a woman.'

'Could it have been the other driver's fault?'

'When the paramedics breathalysed me I was well over the limit and I couldn't walk in a straight line. Maybe the other guy was in the same kind of shape, I don't know. If I'd been sober I'd have approached that intersection more cautiously. The police thought it was worth a one-year ban but that doesn't matter because I won't be driving any more.'

'Your wife died instantly?'

'Yes.' His question made me see Jennifer as she looked after it happened, her face turned towards me, her eyes closed, her mouth open. Why did he need to know how long it took her to die?

'And now you see her face as she died and you're haunted by it?' he continued.

'Yes.' I considered planting my fist in *his* face; if he lowered his head I'd probably break my hand.

'And you wake up in the morning hating yourself?'

'I go to bed hating myself and I get up hating myself, and I hate myself in between, OK?'

'But it was an accident, right?'

'It was an accident but I made it happen.'

'How did you make it happen?'

'I told you: by drinking too much.'

'Did you know that you were going to be driving?'

'Yes.'

'So then why did you drink too much?'

'Lots of people do.'

'That's not a good enough answer. Did you know that drinking would impair your judgement and your reflexes when driving?'

'Sometimes I drive better when I'm a little over the limit.'

'That's what I mean by impaired judgement. Let me put it another way: if you were driving when you had too much to drink, was it really an accident?'

'What are you getting at?'

'There aren't really that many accidents, are there? If you do Thing A that makes Thing B happen, there's no reason to be surprised, is there?'

'Are you saying that I wanted to kill my wife?'

'I'm saying we need to look at what came before the accident.'

'Like what?'

'Like how were things between you and your wife.'

'Is this how you get your jollies or what?'

'This is how we find out what makes things happen.'

'Right. Well, Doc, I think your time is up. Bye bye.' I got up and walked out. Looking back on it later I understood that I didn't really want to know all there was to know about the accident. After a while I got used to my guilt.

Nonetheless I was hoping, with time, to get her death off my back, but it was behind me whichever way I turned. At first I'd been like a parent to it but gradually it became the parent and I the child. When would I grow up and move out of its house? I rubbed my bat tattoo and remembered with embarrassment that I had done it in the expectation that my life was going to change. So far the only change was that I felt more confused than before.

More and more I found myself at the Church of St John's in the North End Road. That smooth fibreglass Jesus had begun to pull me; the idea of someone's dying for our sins was much in my mind. What a lot of big and little sins there were to die for! How could one man handle all of them? But of course that was his thing, that was what made him special. I wished it were a system I could believe in.

It was a damp and foggy November morning with a chill in the air. The fog made everything more personal, as if it were taking me aside to tell me a secret. I was leaning on the church railings and looking at Christ when the John Smith drinker who'd asked me what I wanted from Jesus appeared. I wondered what my answer would be if he asked the same thing again.

'Getting any messages?' he said.

'Not so far. The last time we spoke you quoted Psalm 137.'

'I remember.'

'You said there was a lot of Babylon around here but what Zion do you remember? If you don't mind my asking.'

He shook his head. 'Right now that remembered Zion is all I've got and it isn't something I show around. Haven't you got one of your own?'

Again the smells of oil and metal, cigarette smoke and Jack Daniel's came to me with my father at his work-bench under the light of the green-shaded bulb. Is that my Zion? I thought. Is that all there is? Nothing since my boyhood? I tried to see Jennifer's face and couldn't. The John Smith man was watching me with his head cocked to one side. 'Yes,' I said, 'I've got one. My name's Roswell Clark. What's yours?'

'Abraham Selby.' We shook hands. 'Zion is what you think there's no end of when you have it, then all of a sudden it's gone and there wasn't really that much of it.'

'Can I quote you?'

'Any time. Now I need to think about what I just said. I'll see you.' He went back to the low-budget drinking community and found himself a place to sit on the low wall around the trees. He couldn't be too badly off, I reflected, if he found it worthwhile to think about what he said.

I stood there silent in Babylon while the fog kept me private. There was in the damp chill a smell of freshness and change. The *Passacaglia and Fugue in C Minor* came into my head and of course it brought with it the gorilla and the woman I'd made for Adelbert Delarue. I moved my mind away a little and let images without words come to me. I saw my hand making sketches but I couldn't see what the sketches were. I saw the tools on my workbench; I saw the sheds at Moss & Co, the measured forests of timber, the baulks of lime. I heard the whispering silence.

16

SARAH VARLEY

That hand would not let go of me. That a remnant of a masterfully carved crucifixion should be among the rubbish in that box was unsettling; this fractional representation of real suffering had some importance and it laid on me the responsibility to do the right thing by it. How many miles and how many years had it travelled to get to me?

There's a fair amount of ignorance among market traders; most of us know a little and a few of us know a lot but Dermot and Vernon at the Jubilee Market were the only ones who I thought might have a clue as to the provenance of this fragment. Dermot thought it was Italian; Vernon thought it was German; both of them guessed seventeenth century or earlier.

Sometimes I have little premonitions: I expect to see someone and they appear. Roswell Clark was a woodcarver and I thought he might turn up and shed some light on the crucified wooden hand. About half-past ten suddenly there he was. 'Hi,' I said.

'Hi.' He looked haggard and preoccupied.

'How's it going?'

He shrugged. 'Hard to say.'

'Anything wrong? Bad news of some kind?'

'Oh, no, nothing like that. Nothing especially wrong and no news of any kind.' He looked as if he hoped there'd be no more questions. 'How've you been?' he said.

'Much the same. I've got a recent acquisition I'd like to show you.' I took the hand out of the box under my table and held it out to him. He stepped back, folded his right forearm over his stomach, leant his left elbow on the back of his right hand, and rubbed his chin thoughtfully with his left hand while regarding me suspiciously.

'Was it something I said?' I asked him.

'No,' he said. He was still looking at me. 'Do you ever get the feeling that the world is trying to tell you something?'

'Frequently, and mostly I don't know what the message is.'

'That's how it is with me.' He took the wooden hand from my hand. 'Where'd you get it?'

'At an auction.' I never say too much about my sources when I'm surrounded by fellow traders. 'It was in a box of treen.'

'What's treen?' He held the piece to his nose and sniffed it.

'Small wooden articles; I got a whole box of things in a lot I paid forty-five pounds for. Can you tell anything by smelling it?'

'No. Anything else of interest in the box?'

'No. I'll get my money back but that's about all unless that hand is worth something. Any idea where it comes from?'

'I'm not any kind of expert but I've seen a hand like this in a photo of a crucifixion by Tilman Riemenschneider. Do you know his work?'

'No, I've never even heard the name till now. German? Austrian?'

'German, born in Heiligenstadt in 1460. The crucifixion this reminds me of would probably have been done between 1500 and 1520. One of the experts at Christie's or Sotheby's would be able to tell you more.'

'If this fragment *is* by Riemenschneider, how valuable might it be?'

'I've no idea, really. Since it's only the hand and you can't show where it's from and when and for whom it was done I shouldn't think you'd get much for it.'

'I don't know why I asked; I wouldn't want to sell it; all the same, I don't feel too comfortable having it around.'

'Why not?' While we were talking the usual scattering of buyers and lookers were busy picking things up and putting them down. The buskers in the Apple Market were doing *La Traviata*, that aria that she sings after her first meeting with Alfredo, '*E strano!*'. So young and beautiful and doomed to die so soon! The sky was grey and it had begun to rain.

'I don't know,' I said. 'It's what it is and it seems to require something of me.'

'What?'

'I don't know. Maybe it wants to be with you.'

He stepped back as if I'd made a grab for his private parts. 'What made you say that?'

'I don't know. You're a woodcarver, you're sort of related to whoever did this hand.'

'Great, and what will it require of me?'

'I have no idea. Nothing beyond your capability, I'm sure.'

'There you go again!'

'There I go again what?'

'Making gnostic statements.' He seemed quite bothered.

'Gnostic statements! I've never been accused of that before. Discuss.'

We were interrupted by a woman of sixty or so: long white hair in a ponytail and black leather motorcycle gear. She picked up a delicate ruby necklace ticketed at one-fifty. 'What's your best price on this?' she said.

'I can do one-twenty-five.'

'Done.' She took a wad of banknotes out of a black leather pocket and peeled off six twenties and a five. I was going to put the necklace in a bag for her but she shook her head, put the necklace round her neck, and stomped off in her black leather boots. The soprano in the Apple Market began Violetta's Act III aria in which she bids farewell to the dreams of the past: '*Addio, del passato bei sogni ridenti . . .*'

'Why are you crying?' said Roswell as I wiped away the tears.

'I have an arrangement with Verdi: when he does that I do this. We were talking gnostic.'

'Gnostic, yes: you speak as if you know something that I don't know: you say maybe it wants to be with me and it won't require anything beyond my capability. Do you do palm readings too?'

'Goodness! If I'd known you were that easily upset I'd have confined myself to No-Stik statements instead of gnostic ones. Let me buy you coffee and pastry and maybe we can get back to where we were before I went gnostic.'

That got a laugh and he loosened up a little. 'Sorry to make such a scene,' he said. 'It's not your fault – I'm under pressures that make me a little irritable.'

'Not all pressures are bad.'

'Thank you, Dr Varley.'

'No, really – Bach was under pressure to have his music ready for Sunday services, and I should think Riemenschneider was under pressure to deliver his crucifixions by a certain date. Did either of them have a nervous collapse?' I wasn't wagging a finger at him but my voice was.

'Deadline pressure on a specific project is something else; I'm talking about non-specific pressure from people who want you to live up to their expectations.'

'Have you no expectations of your own?'

He looked away, then back at me uneasily. 'You make me feel as if I'm a kid at school and you're the guidance counsellor.'

'Sorry, but I really would like to know.'

He rubbed the back of his head and shuffled one foot backwards and forwards before answering. 'Maybe I've lost my savour.'

He startled me with that one and I couldn't help laughing. 'That's a strange thing to say,' I said. 'I don't think one's savour is that easy to lose. You seem pretty salty to me.'

He shrugged.

'What do you do with yourself when you're not busy with private commissions? How do you spend your time?'

'Hard to say, really: one day follows another and I guess that's all there is. Listen, Sarah, I think it's time for me to go. Thanks for sharing my inadequacy with me.'

'I never said you were inadequate. Don't be angry, stay and have coffee with me.'

'Thanks, but I don't feel up to it.' He turned to go.

'Wait!' I said. 'The hand!' I held it out to him.

'I don't want it,' he said with something like a snarl.

'Maybe it wants you.'

'No.'

'Please, it doesn't belong with me and I don't want to sell it or give it to anyone else. Maybe you don't want it but I need to give it to you. Please?'

He bared his teeth, shook his head, took the hand, put it in his pocket, and walked away as Violetta expired in the Apple Market.

17

ADELBERT DELARUE

Always I underestimate the effect on me of what I do. Did I think I could go to Autun and come back the same as I was before? On my return I looked at everything with eyes on which were imprinted scenes of this time alone and the first time with Solange. And in my ears was still the shouting of the bells.

Victoria tried to interest me in our usual games. She brought out the toys and demonstrated that in my absence new partnerships had been established. By now all four figures had names: the man was Max, the woman Celeste, the mastiff Hector and the gorilla Marcel. Marcel and Max were now an item, while Celeste and Hector had formed a serious attachment, particularly piquant when they performed to the accompaniment of that part of *Swan Lake* where the corps of pretty swanettes come tripping in on point. This failed to enliven me, nor did those special attentions Victoria pressed upon me. I was haunted by the Christ on the tympanum of the west portal of St Lazare.

This outspread, open, entranced Christ, I realised, does not judge: his *existence*, as man and as idea, is a judgement. We pass beneath his hands to the safe sheepfold of God or we fall to the fires of Hell. The Last Judgement is every moment: even this very moment in which Celeste and Hector couple to Tchaikovsky's ballet music and Victoria mouths her devotion. The fires of Hell are not necessarily flames tended by working-class devils with pokers and pitchforks; these fires can equally be the grey and chilly dawn in which one awakes utterly alone beside one's lover.

I think about Roswell Clark and wonder what I expect from him. In the beginning it was clear enough: I was the patron; he was the artist whom I commissioned to make little sexually active crash-dummies: man; woman; mastiff; and gorilla. What is in my mind when I watch these various wooden couplings? What do I think of while Victoria does her best to anticipate my every desire? Sometimes I see mass graves.

Crash Test was a metaphor absurd and profound; I recognised in Clark a talent capable of surprises, possibly of development. Because of the manner in which Crash Test had drawn me to itself it seemed to me that there might be a significance, as yet unknown, in our transactions. I tend to see omens and portents in all kinds of things: if the yolk of my soft-boiled egg is at the top I expect the day to go well.

What does crashing into a wall and flying into pieces signify for me? Mortality, yes – life crashing into death; I have already spoken of that in these pages. Is there more? Is there in me a desire to crash, to go Peng! and fly into pieces? Have I already flown into pieces without the Peng? What did I think my toys would do for me? From depravity does one move on to something higher? Depravity, I think, comes naturally to the human animal. And it is of course more fun than higher things.

As I was saying, in the beginning I was the patron. As

I commissioned the man and woman, the mastiff, and the gorilla, I felt each time that Clark and I were moving closer to something of importance, something that would come from him as his talent demanded more of him. What will it be? The large and the small of it is that I am depending on Roswell Clark for something, I know not what, that will make me feel better than I do now. Money can buy many things, and uncertainty is one of them.

18

ROSWELL CLARK

I had another Jennifer dream. We were on a train, just the two of us. It was the 13.24 to I don't know where. I tried to read our destination on my ticket but the letters wouldn't form a name. I couldn't read the names of the stations we passed through either. There was no one else in our carriage; the lighting was dim and kept flickering; there was rubbish on the tables and all over the floor, empty beer and soft-drink cans rolling about. We were both hungry and we'd expected to get something on the train but there was no announcement about a buffet car. When the conductor came through to punch our tickets I asked him, 'Where are we going?'

He pointed to my ticket and said, 'There.' He looked like the manual-training teacher I'd had in junior high school: large freckled hands with part of his right index finger missing.

'Where's the buffet car?' said Jennifer.

'This train doesn't exist,' he said. 'It's a dream train so there's no buffet car on it.'

'Then how come there's buffet-car rubbish all over the place?' said Jennifer. 'People have been eating and drinking buffet-car food and drink here.'

'Not my problem,' said the conductor. 'Talk to the Transport Minister.'

'If at least there were bar service!' said Jennifer as I woke up. I was hungry and I felt sad because Jennifer had been hungry too and wanted a drink but there was nothing she could do about it because there wasn't a Jennifer any more. Her hunger and her thirst, all of her wants are gone and the world goes on without her except when in the loneliness of death she visits me in a dream.

I had two fried eggs and bacon and toast and jam for breakfast. After my coffee I had a Glenfiddich for Jennifer. Then I had one for me because I was alive and could do that. 'Here's looking at you,' I said to both of us. 'I know I haven't been doing much lately but I'm not idle; I've been making sketches.' Which was true. I didn't want to say anything more about it, even to myself. If there was really anything happening, I'd be the first to know.

My chisels and gouges hung in their pockets, sharp and ready to bite into wood or turn in my hand and plunge into my flesh. 'I know it's hard for you to hang about like this,' I told them, 'but maybe there'll be work for you soon.' I looked around at the workbench, the drawing table, the easel. I didn't want to stay in the house; it was raining and I felt like walking in it.

I put on an anorak and my rain hat, then went to the jacket I'd last worn and got my house keys out of the right-hand pocket. I checked the left-hand pocket without remembering what was in it, then drew back suddenly as my fingers touched the crucified wooden hand Sarah Varley had given me. 'Oh, yes,' I said. 'Thank you very much – it's just what I've always wanted.' I put it on the drawing table, then picked it up again and put it in my anorak pocket.

Then it was like a cut from one scene to another in a film: I was in the North End Road standing by the railings of St John's. It was a real November rain by now, wind spattering the yellow leaves that lay everywhere like fallen hours, days, years. Jesus on his cross was wet and gleaming. Suddenly I felt sorry for my smartass remarks about his fibreglass slickness; he was only a humble artefact, one of millions of images, some of them great and some of them not, reiterating the idea of this one who was called the son of God, crucified large and small, indoors and out, in marble, bronze, wood, and plastic, in wayside shrines and echoing cathedrals and little hand-held crosses, dying twenty-four hours a day for our sins.

The low-budget drinking community was not in its usual place but I had the feeling that Abraham Selby was going to turn up and after a while he did. This time he had an umbrella instead of a can of John Smith.

'Dry day?' I said.

'Every day is not the same,' he replied in such a preacherly way that I almost said Hallelujah.

'A lot of them are, though,' I said.

He nodded. 'Anything today?'

'Messages, you mean?'

'Yes.'

'Were you expecting any?' I asked him.

'Not for me – for you.'

'I wasn't expecting any either.'

'Sure you were.'

'How can you tell?' Under the umbrella and without the John Smith he seemed different from his previous self.

'Takes one to know one.'

'You just said you weren't expecting any messages.'

'Not any more; I've passed my Selby date.'

'But there was a time when you were expecting messages.'

'There was a time when I was expecting a lot of things.'

'Did you get any of them?'

'Some that I wanted and some that I didn't.'

The rain was sometimes drumming on my hat, sometimes slanting across my face; Jesus was on his cross doing his job regardless of the weather and the fingers of the crucified right hand were touching the fingers of my left hand in my pocket; the traffic behind us was hissing and revving and changing gears; the trees were swaying and losing more leaves; Selby was standing there nodding his head as if agreeing emphatically with what he'd just said and I was waiting for him to continue.

'The other day in *The Times*,' he said at length, 'in my local dustbin, I saw that Maria Callas's underwear was being sold at auction. I used to have a lot of her records. You look surprised.'

'I thought you were going to say more about what you expected and what you got.'

'Not today. Right now I'm thinking of God sitting up there in his office.' He tilted his umbrella back to look up at where the rain was coming from; he was in preacher mode now. 'Yes, brother, he's sitting up there in his office . . .'

'Hallelujah,' I couldn't help responding quietly.

Selby nodded several times. 'Maybe he's watching the world on closed-circuit TV. He's looking at war and famine, fire and flood; he's looking at rape and murder and unemployment and people sleeping rough . . .'

'He sees it all,' I affirmed.

'Sees it all,' Selby went on. 'Sees it all and he's smiling because it's his world and he did it his way . . .'

'That's how he did it.'

'Did it his way and there it is, all running smooth and easy. Then he sees Maria Callas's underwear in that auction . . .'

'His eye is on her knickers.'

'His eye is on her knickers and he slaps his thigh and laughs and he says, "You got to hand it to me − I think of everything."'

'Tell it, brother.'

'I just did.'

'When you said *he* and *his*, were you doing it with a capital *h* or a small one?'

'Small. Now I have to go home and think about this.' Like a Punch-and-Judy man he packed up his little invisible church. 'See you,' he said, and walked away under his umbrella.

'See you,' I called through the rain, but I stayed where I was, looking at Jesus on his cross under that little roof that didn't keep the rain off. '"How shall we sing the Lord's song in a strange land?"' I asked him. I was trying to see his eyes but his face went completely blank. The next thing I knew I was out of the rain, sitting on a floor with my back against a wall. My hat was in a little puddle beside me, the crucified hand was still in my pocket, and the curate, Father John, was bending over me, looking concerned. Evidently I was in the church.

'Are you all right?' he said.

'I'm not sure. What happened?'

'A couple of passersby found you lying on the pavement just outside and brought you in here. Do you know how you came to be lying there?'

'I guess I must have fainted.'

'Has this happened before? Are you subject to blackouts, fits of any kinds? Are you on any medication?'

'No, this was a first and I'm not on any medication.'

'Would you like a cup of tea?'

'Thank you, I appreciate your kindness but I think I'll just go home now.'

'First let's see if you're fully ambulatory.'

I stood up and took a few careful steps. 'It seems I am. Thanks again.' I put on my hat, we shook hands, and I walked slowly out to the North End Road but I didn't go home. I needed time to think but I didn't want to be alone just then so I went to Eustace Road. The rain had stopped for a while and the sky had a heroic look, as in a Dutch seventeenth-century marine painting with ships and small craft in heavy seas. I had by now made a fair number of visits to Dieter Scharf but Eustace Road, the inanimate houses of it, always looked at me with suspicion.

Scharf's stern-looking housekeeper had turned out to be quite an amiable woman whose name was Martha. When she saw me she said, 'You look all *verschwiemelt*. Go to Dieter in the workshop; I bring you black coffee and maybe some *Marillenschnaps*, yes?'

'Yes, please. *Vielen Dank!*'

As soon as I opened the basement door I got a whiff of the Dieter Scharf workshop smell: electrical wiring, oiled metal, solder, and cheap cigars. It wasn't quite the same as my father's workshop but it was close enough to make me feel cosy and comfortable. There in the darkness was the bright jumbly island of his work-bench under the green-metal-shaded bulb; and there was Dieter wreathed in vile blue smoke with his invisible charcoal-burner's hut around him and a goblin-haunted forest in the shadows. He was sixty-three, so he wasn't quite old enough to be my father and there was no Jack Daniel's but I always felt safer in his workshop than in my own.

'*Wie geht's?*' he said. He had begun little by little to bring simple German words and phrases into our conversation.

'*Gut,*' I replied, '*und dir?*' Because we had quickly reached the familiar pronoun.

'*Man lebt,*' he said. 'One lives, but from now until the new year I keep my head down and wait for the holidays to go away. I think perhaps there was a fourth wise man and he saw what was coming and stayed home.'

'Do you do anything for Christmas?'

'I drink very much and read Morgenstern until it's over.'

'Who's Morgenstern?'

'German poet, born 1871, died 1914. Good flavour, very sharp, very funny.' From a shelf over the work-bench he took down a volume with a lot of mileage on it and let the book fall open where it would. 'Listen to this – just take in the sound of it: "*Der Werwolf: Ein Werwolf eines Nachts entwich von Weib und Kind und sich begab an eines Dorfschullehrers Grab und bat ihn: 'Bitte, beuge mich!'*" That's only the beginning of the poem. This is about a werewolf who one night goes from his wife and children to the grave of a village schoolmaster and says to him, "Decline me!"'

'Decline?'

'Declension is what he wants. He wants to know the genitive and the dative and so on for *Werwolf.* The dead schoolmaster can only decline *Werwolf* in the singular but the werewolf wants the plural so his wife and children can be included. When the schoolmaster can't do it the werewolf cries, he has tears running down. But he accepts this and he thanks the dead schoolmaster and goes home.'

At this point Martha came down the stairs with black coffee

and *Marillenschnaps* for Dieter and me. 'Get a glass and have one with us, Martha,' he said.

'*Nein, danke*, I have still the shopping to do. If I drink now you don't get your frog-in-the-ditch for supper.'

'Toad-in-the-hole,' said Dieter.

'Whatever,' said Martha. 'Don't drink too much. The last time I schlepped you up the stairs I put out my back.'

'We drink to your back and also your front, Martha,' said Dieter as he poured for us and we raised our glasses. '*Zum wohl!*'

Martha wagged a finger at him and disappeared upstairs.

'Like this *Schnaps* is Morgenstern,' said Dieter. 'Clears the brain. *Prosit!*'

'Here's looking at you, kid,' I responded. We both sipped delicately but greedily. The *Schnaps* was chilled and it went down like bright and sparkling winters and left me with a cosy fire inside at which to warm myself.

'What do you do about Christmas?' he said.

'I drink very much and read M. R. James.'

'*Mensch!* Look what I have on my bench.' He indicated something I'd been going to ask him about. On a base about four feet long and a foot and a half wide was a spooky little wood with black trunks and branches and dark leaves shadowing a path on which was the figure of a man in black with a very pale face. One shoulder was lifted as if to ward off an attack. Some paces behind him was something that was difficult to see clearly because Dieter had veiled some of the spaces between the trees with scrim cloth. It was a creature draped in white to halfway down its legs which were brown and speckled, the feet very nasty.

'That's from "Casting the Runes",' I said, 'but in the story it's a boy.' There was a collected M. R. James on the work-bench, and I quickly found the lines which I almost knew by heart:

And this poor boy was followed, and at last pursued and overtaken, and either torn to pieces or somehow made away with, by a horrible hopping creature in white, which you saw first dodging about among the trees, and gradually it appeared more and more plainly.

'This I know,' said Dieter, 'but my client wants not a boy but a little man with a pale face. Press the button.'

When I did that, there sprang up from concealed speakers 'Some Day My Prince Will Come'. As if activated by the music, the thing with speckled legs began to hop in the most dreadful way, disappearing and reappearing among the trees as the man tried to double back and lose it. Dieter's use of the scrim cloth was wonderful: the trunks of the trees revolved like the rollers of window blinds so that the action was sometimes obscured and sometimes clearly seen. 'Jesus!' I said as the hopping thing caught up with the man. Everything under the trees went dark as the Disney track continued its sugary vocal. Our glasses were empty and Dieter refilled them for either the fourth or fifth time; they were very small glasses. The fireside corner inside me was the cosiest place I'd been for a long time, and my head felt as if it would ping like crystal if I tapped it.

'Heppy days,' said Dieter.

'Here's mud in your eye,' I replied. Alcohol makes me more American. 'I suppose this is a commission?'

'From a rich American,' he said. 'For this one I get fifteen thousand pounds.'

'Not nearly enough. People are getting fifty thousand

pounds for unemptied chamber pots these days and the pots aren't even new. This thing here is museum-standard work – you should have got at least fifty thousand pounds.'

'What did you get for the gorilla?'

'Thirty thousand.' At this Dieter's lower jaw dropped. I'd paid him twenty-five hundred for the mechanism and motor but that left me with twenty-seven thousand five hundred for a crash-dummy primate that was nothing compared to the whole little horror show he'd put together for fifteen thousand.

'Your millionaire is bigger than mine then,' said Dieter. He shook his head philosophically and poured us both another *Marillenschnaps*.

I looked at the toy again. The sound was off; the dreadful hopping creature had returned to its original position among the trees, the man to his on the path. This scaled-down replication of an imaginary scene held a fascination that was disturbing. I turned from it to St Eustace on his horse on the wall. When I pressed the button the little Jesus appeared between the antlers of the stag and Eustace leapt from the saddle and knelt as before. 'I'm dreaming of a white Christmas,' crooned Bing Crosby.

'Do you ever feel like hopping through the woods and doing what the hopping creature does?' I asked Dieter.

'All the time,' he answered, and raised his glass to me.

19

SARAH VARLEY

Sometimes little good things happen, like a break in heavy grey clouds and a bit of blue sky shining through; I read in *The Times* the other day that a secret buyer had acquired all of Maria Callas's underwear that was being auctioned in Paris and vowed to burn it to save her 'dignity and honour': definitely a bit of blue sky, that.

There's been a lot of rain lately and I'm surprised at how often I find myself on the banks of the Euphrates; that's an operatic allusion, and I can't do many of those because I know very little about opera. Giles and I used to go to the ENO sometimes but I hadn't been for years when Linda gave me a ticket for *Nabucco*; she was going to visit a daughter who was ill and she wouldn't take any money for the ticket. I'll get to the Euphrates shortly.

I wanted to give myself time for a leisurely coffee before the seven-thirty start of the opera, so I left the house at quarter-past six. It was warm for December and raining. The houses and shops were aggressive with Christmas illumination and decorations; the lamps on Parsons Green and the two lantern-like telephone boxes, the figures in ones and twos moving into and out of the lamplight all heightened the singleness of my footsteps. The platform at the top of the station stairs was bustling and festive with people coming and going with shopping bags, and the houses and flats they were coming from or going to were made cosy in my imagination because of the rain all around us.

When I changed to the Piccadilly Line at Earls Court the early evening crush wasn't too bad and I found a seat, took *Middlemarch* out of my bag – I'd first read it years ago – and settled down comfortably with it. I couldn't help shaking my head and smiling at Mrs Cadwallader's remark on page 537 of my Penguin edition: "'We have all got to exert ourselves a little to keep sane, and call things by the same names as other people call them by.'" After a few moments I stopped smiling. I don't care about calling things by the same names as other people but I was wondering whether I'd always called things by the names that were true for me: what I had with Giles, for example. We'd gone to the opera, to concerts, to films; we'd done what lovers do and I'd chosen him as a life partner. He turned out to be a non-finisher, a faller-by-the-wayside. Had I wanted someone I could work on and improve? Was I a faller-by-the-wayside-saver?

Going up the escalator at Leicester Square I passed a young couple kissing on the down escalator and I remembered when Giles and I had done that on that same moving stairs.

VAUXHALL WORKERS' SHOCK AT CLOSURE, said the *Evening Standard* headline as I came out of the station. Over the road Leicester Square presented itself as Hell in modern dress, swarming and throbbing, its noise made visible in neon and glittering lights. BEST COMEDY, flaunted the sign under the marquee of Wyndham's Theatre on this side of Charing Cross Road. RICHLY PERCEPTIVE, SPARKLING, boasted the critical quotes hanging there. '*Big Issue*,' said a vendor.

Although I always exert myself to keep sane I'm not always sure that I'm calling things by the same names I used to call them by. GABY'S DELI in glittering metallic letters over the yellow awning – was that the name when Giles and I had hot salt-beef sandwiches there? Est. 1965, so only the sign was new. The tastes came back to me of the too-muchness of salt beef, mustard, rye bread, beer, and the simple pleasure of gluttony. No one had ever heard of mad cows back then.

Is it a sign of growing old, I wonder, when the faces coming towards you in the street are full of stories that you don't want to know? Here now were Cecil Court and Lipman & Sons Formal Wear, reassuringly itself and staunch through the years with correct attire for morning and evening. As I walked through the rain towards St Martin's Lane in the lamplit and quickstepping darkness the shops on both sides held out their racks and windows to me, entreating me to buy old books, rare books, prints and maps, antiques old and new, ephemera, esoterica, and works on the occult. Stuart and Watkins! No, now they were just Watkins Books. Had they always had ibis-headed Thoth on their signboard? That's where I bought my copy of *I Ching* and Giles bought his Tarot cards. *Living with Zen* was currently being featured in their windows. It was always difficult for me to walk past the maps at Edward Storey's Ltd without buying one; I can't help feeling there's a place they want to show me but I've never taken the chance for fear of falling off the edge of my world. There were prints as well, and the people bent over them assumed, as always, the postures in which Daumier painted print-browsers. I suppose the postures for every action are always there and successive generations fall into them.

This rainy evening in Cecil Court seemed always to have been there with its pavement glistening under the many footsteps; even when the sun is shining Cecil Court is a reservoir of yesterdays, a pool of grey light in which moments long gone surface like carp rising to be fed.

St Martin's Lane, of course, was all go, with a posh new anonymous hotel and CAFÉ ST MARTIN'S PIZZA confronting me when I left Cecil Court and crossed through the taxis to the English National Opera side. Linda had recommended Aroma coffee so I wove through the pedestrian traffic until I saw it just before the ENO.

The place was crowded but I found a seat at one of the little tables and the coffee was very good indeed. Some of the people there were clearly bound for *Nabucco*; a few even had programmes. Most of the ENO opera-goers don't dress up as much as the punters at the Royal Opera House; I remember from the past that they tend to laugh very loudly at the feeblest joke or any naughty word and to shout 'Bravo!' as much as possible, even to the women. At the table next to mine there was a couple talking about *Nabucco*. The woman was a handsome lady in her fifties with hennaed hair; the man was in his seventies, short and bearded, with spectacles; they had a married air.

'This is a David Pountney production,' said the man. He had an American accent.

'I know,' said the woman. 'There'll probably be trench coats.' Very slight German accent.

'What do you think,' he said, 'Berlin or Moscow in the thirties? Beijing in the eighties?'

'Whatever. Plus lots of children in smaller trench coats. Have you looked it up in the opera book?'

'No. I've heard the chorus of the Hebrew slaves at one time and another but that's all I know about *Nabucco*. I was just now trying to remember which Orpheus had the naked dancers standing on rocks and turning around slowly.'

'Not the Monteverdi; that was the one with the twitchers.'

'I know that. Was it Gluck? *Orpheus and Eurydice?*'

'That's the one. I don't think you'll get any naked dancers tonight.'

'You win some, you lose some. Read any reviews?'

She looked thoughtful. 'Yes, and I think somebody loved it and somebody hated it but I don't remember who said what. Any idea what time it's over?'

'The brochure said five past ten, so figure it's always a little later plus curtain calls – we might get out of there by ten-twenty, and with luck we'll be home before eleven-thirty. I'm looking forward to the herring salad.'

'Me too. Have you finished your coffee?'

'Yes, let's go so there's time for the loo before we take our seats.'

They got up, took their shoulder bags, and made for the door. He was in jeans, large autonomous-looking black boots, black polo-neck, blue crocheted waistcoat, a scruffy green anorak, and one of those little tweed hats old duffers wear; she was taller than he and more elegant in a beaded fifties cardigan, a narrow snakeskin-patterned coat, a long black skirt, and black boots. I wondered what their life was like. He was not an impressive figure but despite his age he didn't seem retired. How did they get together? When I see a good-looking woman with a much older man I tend to assume that money or fame must have been the attraction. Why do any two people get together? What about Giles and me? I still remember that he looked at me the way a man who knows horses looks at a horse; and how did I see him? As a man who needed to be improved by me. Oh dear.

The scaffolding on the outside of the Coliseum darkened the entrance and made it seem a place where a password might be required; the lobby was thick with people queueing for tickets while others went inside. At the Jubilee Market and other venues I find crowds invigorating but elsewhere they make me uncomfortable. Not reasonable of me but there it is. I bought a programme and made my way past various knees to the centre of the first row of stalls, seat A15; Linda is very short and doesn't like to sit behind people who block her view.

The interior of the Coliseum was in the grip of scaffolding that seemed to have paused in the act of consuming the place. There were elevated walkways on both sides and behind me, with ladders and planking for ascents and descents, entrances and exits. There was a platform over the left side of the orchestra pit with chairs and music stands on it. The curtain was painted to resemble a torn scroll with Hebrew lettering. The house was filling up rapidly with the usual sound of a swarming audience: people with tickets on the right started from the far left and worked their way east past all the knees, handbags, umbrellas, canes and coats between them and their seats, while those with seats on the left started from the far right and worked their way west.

Having squashed my coat and hat under the seat I opened my programme at random and found Psalm 137 staring me in the face:

By the rivers of Babylon, there we sat down, yea, we wept when we remembered Zion.

We hanged our harps upon the willows in the midst thereof.

For there they that carried us away captive required of us a song; and they that wasted us required of us mirth, saying: Sing us one of the songs of Zion.

How shall we sing the Lord's song in a strange land?

If I forget thee, O Jerusalem, let my right hand forget her cunning.

If I do not remember thee, let my tongue cleave to the roof of my mouth; if I prefer not Jerusalem above my chief joy.

Remember, O Lord, the children of Edom in the day of Jerusalem; who said, Rase it, rase it, even to the foundation thereof.

O daughter of Babylon, who art to be destroyed, happy shall he be, that rewardeth thee as thou hast served us.

Happy shall he be, that taketh and dasheth thy little ones against the stones.

There were tears rolling down my face. I dug a tissue out of my bag and wiped my eyes and blew my nose. Years ago when I read straight through the Old Testament and the New I did all of the psalms at one go, since when I've looked at a few now and then, but the only one that sticks in my mind is 137. It isn't associated with any person, place, or event in my past – it's just that it gets to me in various ways at various times; there is a kind of spell in those words. 'By the rivers of Babylon . . .' Yes! Who has not been captive in some kind of Babylon and hanged his or her harp on a willow, unable to sing in a strange land? The psalm begins with lyrical lamentation and ends with a bloodthirsty cry for vengeance; the exiles so full of pity for themselves have none for the infants of Babylon whose brains they hope will be spattered on the stones. And yet! And yet words have an amoral power: put certain ones together in a particular way and people will weep or dance or pick up a paving stone or a gun or whatever comes to hand.

When had my Zion been? I saw afternoon sun slanting on the grasses of Maiden Castle; there were sheep safely grazing; the grasses stirred in the winds of the long past and the footfalls of ghosts. 'These Iron Age earthworks,' Giles had explained, 'were made to conform to the shape of the hills they were on, to make use of the earth forces. Speaking of which, in the aerial photographs, the system of ramparts and ditches in the eastern entrance remind me of a vagina.' 'So many things do,' I said. The sun was behind him, and his wind-ruffled hair had a golden penumbra.

'Nebuchadnezzar,' said an American accent to my left. It was the man from Aroma. 'Nabucco is the Italian version.'

'You needn't shout,' said his wife, 'I can hear you quite well. Nebuchadnezzar had the feet of clay?'

'The idol he dreamt of,' said the man as the lights dimmed. The curtain had gone up without my noticing and there were musicians on the platform over the orchestra pit and other musicians on the stage, not exactly trench-coated but in grotty combinations of outdoor wear and military surplus. The conductor had forgone the usual spotlit entrance and was onstage in his shirtsleeves conducting the overture. Were there already other people onstage? I can't remember – the whole thing had taken me unawares and I hadn't even looked at the cast or the synopsis in my programme. The overture was a take-charge affair that affectingly foreshadowed, from mood to mood, what was to follow; as it went on I was startled to realise that I knew the part I was hearing: it was an instrumental version of the chorus of the Hebrew slaves. I suppose it's one of those things that everyone knows without necessarily knowing what opera it's from.

Now I could see that the elevated walkways went across the back of the stage as well, continuous with the ones on both sides and behind me. There was a great deal of traffic on these, and when both Hebrews and Babylonians were in military garb I couldn't always tell which soldiers I was seeing. The staging was adapted to the exigencies of the refurbishment and had a rather startled *ad hoc* look that added to the excitement of what was definitely a rouser – a very dynamic production with a soprano, Lauren Flanigan, who seemed a whole *risorgimento* in herself. Part of my pleasure in her performance was a response to her own keen enjoyment of the role of Abigaille, who turned out not to be Nabucco's daughter; when Nabucco goes mad she usurps the throne and arranges the execution of the real daughter, Fenena, a mezzo who has a Hebrew boyfriend. Nabucco, however, reclaims his sanity and his kingdom, renounces Baal, and saves Fenena and the Hebrews. Abigaille then does the decent thing and takes poison in the very best operatic tradition. This of course is not a complete or coherent synopsis. I was not equally attentive to all the principals and events – my interest was mainly in Abigaille and Fenena. Anne Mason was a spirited and touching Fenena, and I was greatly relieved when she was rescued by the newly converted Nabucco. I found the whole production highly satisfying, but for me the main event was the famous chorus of the Hebrew slaves in Scene Two, Part Three, *The Banks of the Euphrates*; we had arrived at the rivers of Babylon and I broke out in goosepimples.

Since then I've bought a recording of *Nabucco* sung in Italian, and I've been listening to that chorus as Verdi heard it. '*Va, pensiero, sull'ali dorate . . .*' it begins, [Fly, thought, on wings of gold . . .] and goes along quietly with the spirit building in it until it swells into '*Oh, mia patria si bella e perduta!*' [Oh, my country so lovely and lost!]. By the time it reaches '*Arpa d'or dei fatidici vati, perche muta dal salice pendi?*' [Golden harp of the prophetic seers, why dost thou hang mute upon the willow?] I'm ready to grab Giles's cricket bat and head for the nearest ramparts. Small wonder that it became emblematic of the spirit of the *risorgimento* and was sung spontaneously by the crowds following Verdi's funeral procession through the streets of Milan.

That was the music in my head when I left the Coliseum, and with it came Psalm 137 and my remembered Zion. The rain had stopped, and after I crossed St Martin's Lane in the intervals between taxis and was once more in the darkness of Cecil Court I saw again the afternoon sunlight on the wind-stirred grasses of Maiden Castle. How shall I sing the Lord's song in a strange land? I thought. But then, really, that's what life is, isn't it: a strange land.

20

ADELBERT DELARUE

Whichever way you turn, your mind comes with you. To take the boy out of the Jesuits, that is possible, but to take the Jesuits out of the boy, that is not possible. In a dream I was stone, yes, chiselled by Gislebertus. I was one of the sinners on the tympanum of the west portal of the Cathedral of St Lazare. Is this all there is? I thought. If so, nothing much can happen. But just then two gigantic stone hands gripped my head and lifted me by it and I was eye to eye with Christ. 'Well,' he said, 'what have we here? It looks like a von Peng sort of sinner.'

'Delarue,' I said faintly.

'Whatever,' said Christ. From his garment he took out a much-used stone notebook and a stub of stone pencil. As he leafed through the pages it was like the riffling of tombstones. He frowned, licked the point of the stone pencil, and made a note. 'I regret to see,' he said, 'that you have done business with some people not of the best, have you not, my old?'

'That was my father, Gottfried von Peng,' I said. 'Of his business affairs I know nothing.'

Again Christ flipped through the stone pages. 'Ah,' he said, 'did you inherit from him?'

'Well, yes,' I said.

'It goes,' he said. 'With the money, the sins.'

'That hardly seems fair.'

'What can I tell you?' he said with a smile. 'Would you like to hear chapter and verse of how you've spent your time and your money since coming into your inheritance? Shall we speak, for example, of lewd toys?'

'You must have a great many demands on your time,' I said. 'How can you concern yourself with such trifles?'

'There are no trifles,' said Christ. 'There are no little things; everything is big. Dare one hope that when you wake up you'll try to . . .' At this point the great stone hands let go of me and I lost the rest of his words in the rush and roar of warm air as I fell.

'Do better?' I shouted as I woke up.

'Didn't I do it the way you like?' said Victoria. 'Wasn't it good for you?'

'Quiet!' I said. 'I'm trying not to lose the dream.'

'Aren't we all?' said Victoria.

21

ROSWELL CLARK

Imagine a man climbing out of his office window and standing on a ledge forty storeys above the street. He's about to jump and maybe he asks himself, 'How did I get here?' It's a heavy question but the answer is very simple: he got here because one thing led to another and this is jump time.

Since finishing the gorilla I'd made a second trip to Tiranti's for bigger chisels and gouges, a lignum vitae mallet, bench screws, and two adzes, one with a curved edge and one straight. I picked up the straight–edge adze, hefted the weight of it and felt its intention move up my arm. Then I went to Moss & Co for more lime.

The underground station at Hammersmith Broadway was manic with Christmas decorations, as was King Street when I crossed to it. It was raining, which somewhat moderated the visual din and seemed friendly. Walking to Dimes Place with the rain gently screening me from evil influences I felt that things might go well. In Dimes Place the old paving stones glistened their welcome and opened the familiar perspective of sheds in which the timbers and the forest spirits waited. 'Ebony, Iroko, Jelutong and Lime,' I said, 'I'm not sure that I'm ready for what I'm probably going to do.' I touched the fingers of the crucified hand in my pocket as I entered the Lime shed. 'What do you think?' I said to the quiet leaning timbers, the attentive spirits of the wood. 'Please be honest with me.'

Be unsure, they said. Be humble.

'Is that all you have to say?'

That's all there is, they said.

'Thanks,' I said. 'I'll go with that.' I had intended to make a clay model before going to the wood but now I found that I wanted no intermediate steps. I had sketches, I had what was in my head, and I wanted to feel my tools cutting away everything that was not the image in my mind. I went to the office, showed Stuart Duncan various scraps of paper with measurements, did the necessary calculations with him, bought the wood for delivery the next day, and went home.

That evening I watched *Mercy Mission – the Rescue of Flight 771* on video. The events in this story actually happened and the people are real. On a Christmas-Eve morning a young flyer and his partner take off from San Francisco to deliver two used Cessna crop-dusting planes to Sydney. Their Flight 771 is in four stages over the Pacific with stops at Honolulu, Pago Pago, and Norfolk Island. These planes were not designed for long-distance flight and are ill equipped; the whole thing is a bad idea but the pilot and his pregnant wife need the money badly.

All goes well as far as Pago Pago but when they take off on Christmas morning the partner crashes and although he's unhurt his plane is destroyed. He goes home and now our young pilot, who has no long-distance experience, flies on alone. Norfolk Island is a tiny speck on his map and he's navigating by compass and dead reckoning, hoping that he's compensating correctly for crosswinds.

Fourteen hours out of Pago Pago he's a half-hour overdue at Norfolk Island and there's no land in sight. He's lost over the ocean and running out of fuel with night coming on. He calls Auckland but he's not within range of their radar so he's not on their screens; his automatic direction finder is broken and he can't tell them where he is. No search-and-rescue team can find him before he has to ditch; the best Auckland can do is patch him through to a veteran pilot on a New Zealand Air flight from Fiji to Auckland with a planeload of passengers.

Before he can be helped the exhausted young man must be located. Determined to save him from death in the sea, the older man, with unflagging ingenuity, finds him after many tries and leads him to Auckland. By this time our pilot has been flying for more than twenty-three hours. The rescuer lands first; he watches the little Cessna glide in and out of the darkness and the rain with an empty tank; then he half carries the young man out of the plane. I cry every time I see that little plane glide in empty.

Tomorrow when the wood arrived I'd cut pieces to size, glue them as necessary, wait for the glue to dry, and then get started on my first uncommissioned woodcarving.

Tomorrow came, and the wood. I sawed, I glued with Evo-Stik, and I waited until the next day. I was very nervous; the block of lime was screwed to the bench and my tools lay beside it, all of them razor-sharp and just as ready to bite into my flesh as the wood. Something needed to be said or done before I put my hand to the work. Prayer? Would it be right for an atheist to pray? I recalled various times when I'd said 'Please' in matters large and small. 'Please let me get there on time.' 'Please let me not drop this.' 'Please let there be hot water.' Was I talking to the train, the light bulb and ladder, the boiler? To what, then? The wood was waiting with my guide lines pencilled in.

I poured myself a large Jack Daniel's; after all, this was the launch of something. Then I put on Peggy Lee, 'Is That All There Is?'. That didn't do it for me, so I went to Boney M and 'Rivers of Babylon', listened to that track once, then tried Mahalia Jackson singing America's Favourite Hymns, starting with Track 5, 'Just a Closer Walk with Thee'. I imagined her singing with her eyes closed, her hands clasped, joyous and secure in her connection with Jesus. Carried along by her fervour, I let the CD run to its end, then I put on Patsy Cline singing 'Just a Closer Walk with Thee'. A different style but there was nothing lost in the change from one singer to the other: they were both hooked up to something that wasn't there for me. And yet . . .

One more large Jack Daniel's and I took up the mallet and the straight-edge adze. 'Please,' I said to the wood. I struck a tentative blow, the adze slipped and bit me in the leg. It didn't find the femoral artery but there was a lot of blood so I bandaged it as well as I could, pressed down hard on it with my hand, and called a minicab to take me to Chelsea & Westminster Accident and Emergency.

'You've got blood all over your trousers,' said the driver. 'I don't want it all over my car.' I've seen faces like his in the paintings of Hieronymus Bosch but better done.

'Give me five minutes,' I said. I went back into the house, wrapped a towel and several plastic carrier bags around the offending leg, took a couple of turns with ducting tape to hold them in place, grabbed a book for the waiting room, and tried the minicab again. 'OK?' I said. 'No blood.'

'If there is, you'll pay for the upholstery,' said my Samaritan, and off we went.

This being a Tuesday morning traffic was fairly light at Accident and Emergency. I gave one of the receptionists my details and joined the other accidents and emergencies among rumpled newspapers and magazines and Styrofoam cups of coffee and soft drinks. There were two Muslim women accompanied by men and small children, a large man with a MOTHER tattoo on his arm, a youth with his arm in a sling, and a young woman who was reading *Captain Corelli's Mandolin*. Nobody was bloody but me. Outside the Fulham Road provided its usual soundtrack while in the waiting room an atmosphere of truancy and withdrawal from the world prevailed.

The book I'd brought with me was Nabokov's *The Luzhin Defense*. I was at the point where chess had overflowed its boundaries to pervade everything and the grandmaster Luzhin saw the shadows on the floor grouping to attack him when my name was called by the triage nurse in her little cubicle.

'You're quite a package,' she said. She had a Scots accent and looked like short shrift but with a friendly grin. She spread some paper towels on the floor, unwrapped me, and told me to pop off my trousers. 'What happened?' she said.

'I was working on a woodcarving when the adze slipped.'

'Accident-prone, are you?'

'I didn't use to be but maybe I am now.'

She cleaned the wound, which was only oozing now, put on a temporary dressing, and solved the bloody-trousers problem by giving me a hospital dressing-gown and steering me into a cubicle for express stitching by Dr Kohn, a young man who looked as if he knew too much. 'You should get an anatomy book if you want to do the job right,' he said with a straight face. 'You missed the artery by about an inch.'

'Very funny. Do I look suicidal?'

'No more than others I've seen but you never know – a lot of accidents aren't strictly accidental.' He raised his eyebrows and looked at me knowingly.

'Thank you for your input. If I had my notebook with me I'd write that down.'

'Maybe you can remember it.'

'I'll try. Thanks for the stitches.'

A pair of hospital pyjamas was found for me and a plastic bag for my trousers. I phoned for a minicab and went home.

I didn't feel quite ready to pick up adze and mallet again, and although my leg hurt I could walk normally, so after lunch I took myself to the Royal Academy of Art to see *The Genius of Rome* exhibition. This exhibition, drawing on so many museum and private collections, was as remarkable logistically as artistically and was unlikely ever to happen again. Painters from all over Europe who had worked in Rome between 1592 and 1623 such as Rubens, Bril, and van Honthorst were represented along with Caravaggio, Caracci, Saraceni, Gentileschi, and the other native Italians.

A slowly moving procession of eyes met, again and again across the centuries, the eyes of lute players, courtesans and low life, Christ and the Virgin, the penitent Magdalene, and a variety of saints and Old Testament figures. The modernity of the faces was startling – I've seen Caravaggio's gypsy fortune-teller at the cashier's window in Lloyds, d'Arpino's Virgin reading the *Sun* on the District Line, Gentileschi's St Francis selling vegetables in the North End Road, and everybody's Christs everywhere. These many faces of Christ spoke to me and asked questions but for the time being I avoided this dialogue and gave my attention to the landscapes of Paul Bril.

I was much intrigued by a small one, only thirty-two

centimetres wide, oil on copper, *The Campo Vaccino with a Gypsy Woman Reading a Palm.* There were some good-looking Roman ruins in the foreground, middle distance, and far distance. The near ones were in shade, making as it were a proscenium through which to view the far sunlit ones. There were many people and cattle. The figures nearest the viewer were deeply shadowed; the eye moved beyond them to the gypsy, her client, and the others grouped with them, and from them to the further sunlit figures. The campo, the ruins, the trees and sky and the divisions of space, light, and shadow were the main action; the gypsy and her group gave scale and emphasis to the visual planes of near, middle, and far. The colour, although austere and restrained, had a richness about it. If I had been able to stand in the real Campo Vaccino with the ruins and figures arranged as in the picture it would not have had the peculiar charm of the painting because the visual planes would not have been so ordered, so beguilingly presented. Everything in the picture was real but Paul Bril had restaged it so that the eye and the mind of the viewer could better contain it. Yes! I thought, if I could only see my life with the light and shadow and colours of near, middle, and far, I could . . . What?

I smelled honeysuckle and saw Sarah Varley looking at the same picture. 'If only reality could pull itself together like that,' I said.

'I wonder why it is that we like to look at architectural ruins,' she said.

'Maybe looking at them makes us feel that humans can outlast brick and stone.'

'Humans can outlast all kinds of things . . .' She seemed about to say more but she stopped. 'I'll move on,' she said.

'I find it difficult to adjust my viewing pace to anyone else's.' Off she went.

I'm a pretty fast viewer myself and sometimes I saw her nearby but I was careful not to catch up with her. She paused thoughtfully for quite a long time at a painting which I found to be, when I reached it, Artemisia Gentileschi's *Judith Beheading Holofernes*. However dirty the job, it had fallen to Judith to do it and she was equal to it; from the expression on her face you might have thought she was filleting herring.

I liked Leonard Bramer's little oil-on-copper *The Fall of Simon Magus*. A horse and an idle spectator occupied the foreground; beyond them was Peter with a halo, kneeling and putting the whammy on Simon while, some little distance away, Nero watched from his throne. Simon Magus, falling through the dark air above them, his garments fluttering about him, was the smallest person in the picture. Well, he had ideas above his station so what could he expect?

'What an embarrassing comedown for poor old Simon Magus,' said an American accent to my right. It was Peter Diggs, a painter who teaches at the Royal College of Art. He lives close by in Fulham and we bump into each other from time to time.

'No one seems to be taking much notice,' I said. 'He probably thought he was the main character in this scene but he's quite small in the overall picture.'

'Aren't we all?'

'Yes, but sometimes we're smaller than other times.'

He raised his eyebrows at that, then looked at his watch. 'Got time for a coffee after this?'

'Yes.' We went along pretty quickly and were soon in Gallery 8 and the last part of the exhibition. We did the room clockwise, and so came to Caravaggio's *The Madonna di Loreto* before the last wall and his *The Entombment*. The humble pilgrim couple with dirty bare feet, kneeling at the door with hands clasped prayerfully, looked up at the Virgin with the Child in her arms. 'Just imagine,' I said, 'making that pilgrimage to the Virgin and having her answer the door.'

'Her name was Lena. According to one of my books she sat for Caravaggio so often that a notary called Pasqualone became jealous; Caravaggio wounded him in a duel or a fight of some kind and had to get out of Rome so he went to Genoa.'

'With Lena?'

'I don't think so; the book doesn't say.'

'She looks like a woman men might fight over. I wonder if being the Virgin in that painting had any effect on her life; I wonder how she felt about it as she got older.'

'You think, maybe years later, she'd go to the church where the picture was hanging and tell people, "That's me, that's how I used to look."'

I thought she might have done that. 'And after all,' I said, 'she used to be a virgin too.'

'Up to a point, certainly.'

Now we were stood in front of *The Entombment*. Through the galleries I had seen Christ taken by soldiers, mocked, crowned with thorns, shown to the populace, and crucified. His face and body had changed from one painter to the next and even Caravaggio's Christs differed one from the other, but now all these images had mingled and precipitated this heavy mortal residue of the dead Christ being lowered on to a stone slab. His mouth was open, holding a silence.

I needed to be alone after that but I'd said I'd have coffee with Peter so I did. The ground-floor restaurant murmured and clattered around us; the lamps accentuated the dimming of the winter afternoon beyond the windows. 'You're very quiet,' said Peter. 'I think I've come between you and your thoughts.'

'That's all right,' I said. 'They won't go away. How's your work going?'

'Nothing much happening at the moment. My paintings used to come from an emptiness in me; now I've lost that empty space.'

'How did you lose it?'

'It got filled up with Amaryllis.'

'Worse things could happen.'

'Oh, I'm not complaining – I'm happier than I've ever been; it's just that I feel a little strange, like when you come out of a cinema into bright sunlight.'

'Maybe you need mental dark glasses.'

'I'll work on that. There's Seamus Flannery.' He waved to a man carrying a tray. 'Seamus!' he said. 'Come and sit with us.'

Seamus was a pleasant-looking man, bald and somewhat portly. I guessed him to be a few years older than I. He said, 'Hi,' put his coffee and scone on the table, got rid of his tray, and shook hands with me while Peter introduced us. 'That's some exhibition,' he said. 'I'll have to come back two or three more times.'

'Harold would have been here every day making notes,' said Peter. 'Harold Klein,' he said to me, 'an art historian friend of ours who died two years ago.'

'Of a 14 bus,' said Seamus.

'"*Of* a 14 bus"?' I said.

'He stepped in front of it,' said Seamus. 'He and the 14 had a very complex relationship.'

I shook my head in condolence and also to express that there was nowt so queer as folk.

'As I was looking at the paintings,' said Seamus, 'I was thinking of things to say to Harold but there isn't any Harold any more. I wonder if you ever get used to that kind of thing.'

'After a while it stops,' I said, 'and you just shake your head from time to time when you think of how all the days and nights of that person are gone out of the world; what they did, what they said – all gone.'

Seamus gave me a long look. 'Life,' he said, 'is a process of one goneness after another.'

'That includes ideas,' said Peter. 'I'll have to content myself with portraits and nudes for the time being.'

'Yours is a hard life,' said Seamus. 'Try to find what consolations you can.'

'Do my best,' said Peter. He looked at his watch. 'I'm off to meet Amaryllis. See you.'

'What do you do?' I asked Seamus after Peter had left.

'I teach at the National Film School and I write for radio and television. The radio stuff's been on the air; the television hasn't been.'

'Was there a time before you were doing that,' I said, 'when you knew that was what you wanted to do and you made it happen or did you just fall into it?'

'Knowing what you want to do can be like the 14 bus,' said Seamus. 'Sometimes it's a long time coming.' Now it was his turn to look at his watch. 'I must leave now. Nice meeting you.' He shook my hand and left.

'Not just the 14,' I said. But he was gone. I had another coffee and thought about Sarah Varley whom I hadn't seen since *Judith Beheading Holofernes*; I wondered what she did with herself when she wasn't stalling out.

On my way back to Green Park tube station I was thinking

about Peter and Amaryllis. She's not only very beautiful, she's bewitching, like the nymphs in the Waterhouse painting who drowned Hylas; and when I'd seen them together Peter seemed truly bewitched. Now he'd lost the empty space that his paintings came from. That, at least, was not one of my problems – I had more empty space than I knew what to do with.

Back at the studio the lime was waiting for me in that intimidatingly objective north light. The crucified wooden hand lay on the work-bench; I'd thought of putting it up on the wall but I'd hesitated – I didn't want to be pushy. Now I decided that I *would* be pushy so I took some Blu-Tack and fastened it to the wall over the work-bench. 'Anything you can do,' I said, 'will be greatly appreciated.'

The many faces and bodies of Christ were in my mind and I was expecting a long conversation with him but all that came to me was Caravaggio's *Ecce Homo*. He was a typical Caravaggio in physique, very slight, almost girlish. He looked so meek, so submissive, so humble and unpretentious, that I didn't quite know where to put myself with him.

As I faced my glued-together lime once more I found a thought in my mind: *Let the wood come to you.* So I did, and this time the adze didn't bite me.

22

SARAH VARLEY

The world is full of ghosts: not the kind who groan and clank their chains, not even people ghosts, but the ghosts of the touches of hands on what has been used, worn, handled. Might it be a kind of metaphysical DNA, so that from the touch of a woman's hand on a necklace, a man's hand on a knife, the whole person might be called into being? Indeed, has the whole person ever ceased to be, ceased entirely?

Market trading is not a spiritual pursuit but maybe there is nothing that hasn't got a spiritual side. All of us at our stalls selling the oddments of unknown lives, tarnished medals, broken watches, cloudy mirrors – are we not extending those lives beyond their deaths?

The wooden hand that I gave Roswell Clark, whose was the hand that carved it, whose ghost-touch still lingers on it? Will it let go of me now that I'd passed it on? Somehow I doubt it. Will it get a grip on him? Why do I get involved with unfinished men? Not a romantic involvement but I can feel myself willing him to do something, to make a big step forward. And he's not eager to make that step. What can I say? I'm sorry about this.

I don't think about Roswell Clark all the time; there are

other things on my mind. I was greatly relieved to read in *The Times* that the Pope has apologised to the Greeks for the sack of Constantinople in 1204 by the Crusaders. Elsewhere I saw that the German industrial giant, von Peng International Industries, had finally yielded to the demands of surviving ex-slave labourers. VPI was going to pay them each three thousand pounds while pointing out that the claims of the ex-slave labourers were not altogether justified by the quality of their work; VPI had paid the SS three Reichsmarks per day for each unskilled concentration-camp inmate, four for skilled ones, and one and a half for children; these costs and the compensation were both considered excessive by von Peng International but in the interests of leaving the past behind they were doing the handsome thing. Following on this report came the news that VPI was being restructured, their munitions, industrial chemical, telecommunications, steel-making, oil refining, and pharmaceutical divisions being decentralised under new management; this not surprisingly wiped a good deal of value off VPI shares but somehow the world staggers on and presumably VPI still has a bob or two with which to continue its many enterprises. VPI's gallantry doesn't quite rank with that of the gentleman who bought Maria Callas's underwear and burnt it but it's better than a poke in the eye with an electrified fence.

23

R. ALBERT STREETER

Hi. How you doing? This is R. Albert Streeter speaking, the same who was only a short time ago Adelbert Delarue. There was Delarue in Paris, now Hopla! here is Streeter in the Big Apple. The past is behind us. I am now an American billionaire. Big hat, much cattle, as we Yanks say. It goes; life goes on wherever it goes.

As in the song, so with me: the fundamental things do not change as time goes by. I have long been a patron of the arts and now I have in mind to make a larger commitment than before: yes, I think of opening a museum in London. I have acquired a first-class modern building designed by the internationally famous architect Wolfgang Krumm; with some alterations it will soon be ready for an exhibition of exciting and provocative works by artists competing for the R. Albert Streeter Prize of fifty thousand pounds. Folsom Bray, who was Director of the Post-Modern Gallery, will be Director of the R. Albert Streeter Museum and he will be as a chair for judges of suitable augustness. It is my especial desire to encourage artists whose talent has not yet been recognised and I hope there will be many interesting entries.

So, this ends my first report from the Big Apple, where the natives are always restless and the banks are friendly.

24

ROSWELL CLARK

As I worked I asked myself from time to time, 'Why am I doing this?' Because it seems to want me to, was the only answer I could think of. I let the wood come to me and as I progressed safely from adze to chisel and gouge I watched my blades cutting away whatever wasn't the it that I was doing. Or maybe it was doing me.

In *The Times* this morning there was a tiny little item from Bangalore. The people of Karnataka, it said, are worshipping a one hundred-tonne rock that fell off the back of a truck. This rock was on its way to a temple where it was going to be carved into an image of the monkey-god Hanuman. Every time I think of that I shake my head and smile. Very perceptive, those Karnatakans.

25

SARAH VARLEY

Christmas went away eventually, and by the middle of January London was functioning more or less fully. The new year seemed a thin and dreary thing but possibly that was post-Christmas depression.

I hadn't talked to Roswell Clark since the Royal Academy, and that hadn't really been a conversation. I was mentally leaning forward to help him uphill – I felt that he was climbing *some* kind of hill, perhaps pushing a big rock ahead of him, but I didn't know what the hill was and I didn't know what the rock was. What did he do with his time? 'Private commissions' was what he'd told me and that was all he'd told me. I wanted to see for myself what he was doing but I didn't know where he lived and I didn't have his telephone number. I'd seen him at the V & A, Covent Garden, and the Royal Academy. This being a Saturday I wasn't at the Jubilee Market but it was my guess that he avoided that and the other two places on weekends.

Whatever he was doing, why did it matter so much to me? My first impression of him was that he was a failer but were my first impressions to be trusted completely? My experience with Giles had left me feeling that I was attracted to men who needed improving. Was I attracted to Roswell Clark? Not really, I told myself, but I couldn't help being curious about him.

I had the feeling he might be local, near rather than far. This was a free Saturday; I could do what I liked. I put on a coat and a woollen hat and went out with no particular destination in mind but wondering if I might run into him. The day was dismal, cold and grey. For no reason at all I crossed Parsons Green and paused at the White Horse pub. The tables outside were empty; inside there were only a few people. It was a little after three and I don't usually drink that early in the day but I got a glass of Merlot and took it over to a table.

A young couple came in; the woman sat down at a nearby table while the man went to fetch the drinks. She was very pretty, nice figure, wearing tight jeans and a loose Fair Isle pullover. She looked a little truculent. What have you got to look truculent about? I thought. You're young, you're pretty, your whole life is before you.

The man came to the table with two pints, put one in front of her, sat down, and lifted his glass to her but she didn't respond. He was a nice-looking City type and his manner made me think that he was the one who always made an effort to please. It won't help, I thought. 'Well, Hilary . . .' he said.

'Well, what?'

'Are you going to tell me what's bothering you?'

She took a good pull at her pint before answering. 'Our expectations aren't the same.'

'How do they differ?'

'You seem to think we have a basis for a long-term future.'

'What is it *you* think we have?'

'*Had*. It was one of those interim things, and you knew that very well from the outset. You'd have liked there to be more but that's all there was and you've had it, so now it's time for you to move on to the next thing.'

'That's easy for you to say.'

'Right, everything's easy for me, Andrew – that's why I have such a great life. I have to go now.' She got up and walked out, leaving her unfinished pint on the table. Andrew watched her leave, then finished her pint and his, smacked the table once with his hand, and went to the bar for another pint.

Poor Andrew, I thought. I finished my wine and left, shaking my head over the non-easiness of everything. I had things I could have been doing at home but I didn't feel like doing any of them so I wandered down Basuto Road to Eel Brook Common, then over to the Fulham Road where I fetched up at Coffee Republic drinking coffee and accepting the fact that I wasn't going to bump into Roswell Clark.

On Monday morning Roswell appeared at the Jubilee Market, looking as if he'd been dragged backwards through a very thick hedge. 'Well, here I am,' he said as if he knew I'd been looking for him. I could feel myself blushing.

'What's up?' I said.

'Well, I've done something,' he said, 'OK?'

'What are you talking about?'

'You've wanted something from me, haven't you? You forced that wooden hand on me because you knew it would start working on me, which it did. And now I've done something.'

'What?'

'Would you like to come see it?'

'Yes, I would.'

'When?'

'This evening?'

'When this evening?'

'Where are you?'

'Fulham, SW6. Kempson Road.' He wrote down the address and gave it to me.

'You're quite close – I can be there about eight.'

'Right. See you.' And he was gone so quickly that it almost seemed I'd imagined the whole thing but there was the address in my hand.

For the rest of the day my mind was busy with what Roswell had said about my wanting something from him. I'm always surprised when things I say or do have an effect on people, and I was flustered by his words but not displeased. I couldn't help putting out I-want-to-improve-you pheromones and he had responded appropriately.

Sometimes I observe myself as from a distance doing this or that and it isn't what I usually do but I've learned not to ask myself too many questions. I left the Jubilee Market at three, took my trolley and rucksack and shoulder bag home, went to Marks & Spencer at Marble Arch, bought a pair of peach-coloured silk knickers with lace inserts, went home, had a long shower, dabbed on some Ma Griffe, tried on three or four outfits, and finally settled on a navy Jean Muir and a pink cashmere cardigan that I got at a charity shop. With black tights and high-heeled black boots. 'Do you want to talk about this?' said my mirror self.

'No,' I answered. I had a cup of tea and scanned *The Times*, in which it was reported under the line ORKNEY'S GIFT TO EROTICISM:

The erotic combination of suspender and stocking that launched a million pin-ups was patented in 1896 by two young islanders who saw the potential in an idea for holding up baggy farm overalls. Andrew Thomson and James Drever, 22, apprentice tailors, went to California and lodged a patent for 'a clasp serving to secure the stocking'.

Giles sometimes, not as often as he'd have liked, talked me into wearing suspenders and stockings for him; he said that the division of female flesh by straps or harness of any kind excited him. Now he and his needs were no longer part of the world and I was in tights. I shook myself and looked at my watch: quarter to eight.

From Doria Road to Kempson is a short walk past Parsons Green and across Eel Brook Common. The air was cold and still with a feeling of impending snow. The street lamps, the lights in windows everywhere, and the people who passed me all seemed part of a silent background that heightened my separateness. I found the house, rang the bell, and the door opened immediately as if Roswell had been standing behind it. 'You're here,' he said.

'Well, that was the arrangement, wasn't it?'

'Sorry, please come in. I'm really glad to see you.'

'Are you all right?' I said. 'You seem a little . . .' I could smell that he'd been drinking but drunk wasn't the word I was looking for.

'I am,' he said. He helped me out of my coat and hung it in the hall. 'You look great,' he said. 'I haven't seen you dressed up before.'

'Thank you. This seemed something of an occasion.'

'I suppose it is, in one way or another. The studio's on the top floor.'

I followed him up the stairs past a living room full of books and not too much furniture, a cosy-looking study, and a very sparsely furnished bedroom. The studio was two storeys high with a skylight; for a moment we stood in darkness looking up at the sky, then Roswell switched on two banks of fluorescent lights and there leapt into view a crucified crash-dummy. 'Oh my God,' I said.

Up there on the cross it looked enormous at first but then I realised it was only life-size. The cross was leaning against the wall as if the figure had just been nailed to it and raised up to hang there until dead. The figure was of pale wood, unpainted except for the usual black-and-yellow discs, the blood from the wound in its side and those in its hands and feet; there was also a little blood from the shiny chromium crown of thorns on its bald and eyeless head. The figure was more elongated than the dummies I'd seen in photographs and on television; this had an El Greco effect that accentuated the pain not visible on the blankness of the face. The cross was of a rough dark wood that heightened the pale vulnerability of the body. There was no INRI.

After the first shock a wave of sadness swept over me; my throat ached and my nose tingled and I thought I might cry but I didn't. This sadness wasn't from the crash-dummy Christ but from thinking of the poorness of spirit that had led Roswell to spend all those hours carving it. His soul must be absolutely skint, I thought, for him to come up with this. The reduction of Christ to a dummy made to crash into the wall of our sins, the stripping of a complex and haunting idea to a simplistic metaphor, made me so sorry for Roswell that my heart opened to him and I wanted to take him in my arms and rock him like a baby. I realised that I was standing there looking gobsmacked and I tried to find something to say.

'Drink?' said Roswell. He seemed calmer now.

'Please.' There was a bottle of Jack Daniel's on a work-bench and I pointed to it. 'That'll do nicely.'

He poured large ones for both of us and we clinked glasses. 'He dies for our sins,' he said, and just for a moment I wondered if he was crazy. I was feeling a little crazy myself. The thing was so in-your-face, so asking for trouble, that I half expected the police to arrive at any moment. 'Is this one of your private commissions?' I said.

'No, this is off my own bat. It just sort of came to me.'

We drank in silence for a while, then I said, 'What are you going to do with it?'

'No idea. I had no plans beyond carving the figure.'

'Can you get it through the door?'

'It comes apart, the arms are pegged into the body and so on. Getting it out of here is no problem but where would I take it?'

Another silence, then I heard myself say, 'Have you thought of exhibiting it?'

'No, I haven't.'

'Why not?'

'This thing that I did, I don't understand it. It's as if my hands had something in mind that they wanted to show me but I haven't figured out what it is. Showing it publicly would seem like betraying a confidence.'

'On the other hand, maybe seeing it on public view would make clear to you what it's about.'

'I suppose that's a possibility.'

'Nikolai Chevorski used to say that it's the viewer who completes a work of art. I think he was right about that.'

'Well, you've viewed it, so now it's complete.'

'You know what I mean — it wants to get out into the world.'

'I don't know, Sarah.'

'You've heard about the new art museum?'

'You mean the American one?'

'Yes, the R. Albert Streeter Museum of Art. There's a competition and a fifty-thousand-pound prize.'

'What, you think I should enter this?'

'Yes.' I was beginning to see prospects opening before him and I was feeling good. 'Yes,' I repeated, 'enter it.'

'You really think I should?'

'Yes. If it's accepted for the show it's bound to get a lot of attention and even if it doesn't win it's likely to make things happen for you.' As I said this I was well aware that he was well aware that I'd given him no response to the piece other than my initial shock and this practical suggestion.

'You want things to happen for me?' he said. My glass was empty and he refilled it, his own as well.

'Are you trying to get me drunk?'

'Yes. You haven't answered my question.'

'What was the question?'

'Do you want things to happen for me?'

'Yes.'

'Why?'

'Should I be honest with you?'

'Are you sure you want to go that far on the first date?'

'Is that what this is?'

'I think so,' and he kissed me. It was a serious kiss and I felt like a twenty-year-old. With forty-four years of experience.

'Maybe I won't be honest with you just yet,' I said.

'Good thinking.' He took me by the hand, switched off the studio lights, and we went down to the bedroom where I saw the little china nutcracker standing at attention on the bedside table, shouldering his sword and grinning with all his teeth.

'Take the evening off,' I said, and turned him to face the wall.

Afterwards, as we lay in each other's arms feeling rather pleased with ourselves, I hummed a bit of the song from *West Side Story*. 'I feel pretty,' I said.

He kissed me in various places. 'You're better than pretty – there's a lot of you and all of it's beautiful.' He went back to his kissing.

'I admire your attention to detail,' I said. 'You make me enjoy being a big woman.'

'Pretty knickers!' he said, picking them up from where they'd fallen.

'They're new. I wore them in case I got knocked down by a bus on the way here.'

'I admire your foresight. Now they're historic.' He climbed over me so he could rub the bat on his left shoulder against the bat on my left shoulder.

'A historic meeting,' I said.

'Destiny, you think?'

'Destiny expands to fill the knickers available for it; that's Varley's Law.'

'I've always been law-abiding, Mrs Varley.'

'Good. Now that we're over the hump, so to speak, can I be honest with you even though it's still the first date?'

'Will it hurt?'

'I'm not sure, but I need to do it.'

'All right, do it.' He wrapped me around him and held me close. 'But first tell me that this isn't all there is.'

'This isn't all there is,' I said with my mouth close to his ear.

'And tell me that you're not going away after you're done being honest.' He was kissing my neck.

'I'm not going away,' I murmured, and kissed him here and there.

'OK, I'm ready.'

'Part of what attracted me to you,' I said, 'was that I could see you needed work.'

'Work as in employment?'

'No, work as in a house that needs work. I'm a man-improver, I can't help it. Will you throw me out now?'

He clasped my bottom firmly with both hands. 'I don't think I can let go of you. Feel free to improve me – I always need work.'

So I worked on him a little and he declared himself much improved. By then we were both hungry but didn't feel like going out so we went down to the kitchen in knickers and T-shirts (he gave me one of his) and Roswell made salami and eggs with oven chips and there was champagne to go with it, three bottles waiting in the fridge.

'You expected to have something to celebrate?' I asked.

'I always keep some chilled in case I get seduced by an ardent woman in silk knickers.'

'Yes, it's good to be prepared for these things.' He had put on a Thelonious Monk CD, and 'Round Midnight' traced its shadowy yesterdays while we ate and drank. The kitchen was a bit ramshackle, with a fluorescent light flickering under the bottom shelf of a unit that had been united in a marriage of convenience with a pine dresser; there were brightly coloured cabinets stuck here and there on the walls, a DIY exhaust fan over the cooker, and a bachelor-not-coping-all-that-well look about the place that warmed my heart. A tidy little spice rack on the wall, however, hinted at a woman's presence. 'You're not married, are you?' I said.

He gave me a startled look. 'Was,' he said. 'She died seven years ago.'

'My husband died in 1993.' Then there was silence as we both looked into the middle distance.

'This table,' said Roswell, caressing that scarred and variously scorched item, 'is a plain deal table.'

'Yes, I can see that.'

'Back in the States I used to read a lot of English authors and the stories often featured plain deal tables. I always wanted one.'

'I understand,' I said. 'A plain deal table is a plain deal: what you see is what you get. You might even say it's a quinsettentially English kind of thing.'

'Quinsettentialism is good,' he said, pouring more Moët & Chandon. I was feeling cosy and uneasy at the same time: cosy because of the Jack Daniel's, the lovemaking, the salami and eggs, and the Moët & Chandon; uneasy because I didn't know where each of us stood in relation to the crash-dummy crucifixion. If it was accepted for the exhibition it would certainly get him noticed and it would likely end up in the collection of some cutting-edge aesthete for whom last week's shocker was, well, last week. What was I going to say if he asked me what I actually thought of it? After the champagne came *Marillenschnaps*, so although my brain felt beautifully crystalline by then I did more nodding and smiling than talking while my critical faculty, like some dreadful hopping creature, pursued me through the dark forest of my thoughts.

Fortunately he didn't ask my opinion on the crucifixion

as art. For the rest of the evening we exchanged histories and got more and more comfortable with each other. We went to bed around three o'clock in the morning, and although I was feeling tired by then the drink seemed to make me wakeful rather than sleepy. For a long time we lay quietly like two spoons, his front against my back. Roswell's breathing sounded wakeful too but neither of us spoke; I think we were both getting used to the idea that maybe we weren't alone any more. We fell asleep after a while and when we woke up each of us found the other still there: nobody had gone away. 'You can look now,' I said to the nutcracker. I turned him around so he could see how things stood and he seemed pleased.

26

R. ALBERT STREETER

Here in the Big Apple I am doing it 'my way'. If one can make it anywhere, one can make it here also. Well, it goes. From time to time a change is good, is it not? In financial matters and also in others. Particularly for the jaded (is there any other kind) hedonist. One tries this and one tries that: sometimes yes, sometimes no.

Through an advertisement in a publication called *Model World*, I have found a most interesting new talent. His name is Dieter Scharf, and he has made for me a miniature realisation of a scene adapted from a story by M. R. James. Victoria introduced me to this writer and reads to me from him. Horror has its erotic aspects and our new toy has given to Victoria and me fresh stimulation. Ah, that dreadful hopping creature! Who knows the manner of its pleasures? 'Some Day My Prince Will Come'! I am now reading H. P. Lovecraft and thinking of Cthulhu rising from the sea out of his dead city of R'lyeh. Cthulhu and Fay Wray? For this I hear perhaps 'The Good Ship Lollipop'. Possibilities of this new direction will not soon be exhausted! I foresee many commissions and so I have started at a lower figure than with Clark.

I am in close touch with Folsom Bray at the R. Albert

Streeter Museum of Art. He tells me there are a great many entries in the competition and I swell with pride at the thought of undiscovered talent that will because of me have its day in the sun. Possibly even at the bank.

Life is good, not always in the same place, but good.

27

ROSWELL CLARK

The R. Albert Streeter Museum of Art at the southern end of Hoxton Square was a misshapen white thing that seemed to have hopped out of nowhere to pounce on the square and rend it from the decent quiet of its pre-modernist past. Already the Lux Gallery near the southwest corner flaunted the glass of its pretensions next to the modest brick front where a blue plaque murmured that James Parkinson, 1755–1824, physician and geologist, had lived there. Rebel Music and Tiger Beer (with a yin–yang logo) carried the trend of change up to the northern end where St Monica's Catholic Church drew back, shaken, from the self-exposure of the new museum visible through the bare winter trees of Hoxton Square Gardens. On the eastern side Apollo Dispatch looked busy and Thomas Fox & Co, Engineering and Transport, had not yet become a coffee shop but letters were falling from its name.

The sky looked ready to snow. The ground was black with artists and their entries all round the square and into the street leading from it. I'd hired a man called Nigel to take my entry in his van to the museum and Sarah had come along to help and to see what kind of talent I'd be competing with. We sat in the back with my brown-paper parcels and timbers that looked as if they'd be more at home in a skip. When assembled, they now had a title: *The One for the Many*. A policeman in a neon-yellow jacket waved us on out of the square to the distant end of the queue and there Nigel dropped us and our burdens and left.

I'd brought along a home-made dolly, a small carpet-covered wooden platform on casters, and with careful stacking we were able to get the figure parcels on it. Sarah took charge of that while I took the timbers of the cross and those of the easel structure that supported it. I paid Nigel, he drove off, and there we were, queueing with people and works that might or might not be the future of what might or might not be Art. The various lengths of wood I was lumbered with were tied together and were quite heavy; the queue was moving very slowly and I dragged my burden with me as we inched along with more stops than starts.

'It might be easier for you if you assembled the cross and put it over your shoulder,' said Sarah.

'Maybe this Easter,' I replied.

Ahead of us in the queue was a tall dark-haired young woman wearing jeans, a mangy Persian lamb coat, a Russian hat of the same material, and something of a lip-piercing nature in her lower lip. Her entry seemed to be the contents of a Boots carrier bag. 'That's yours?' she said, indicating the timbers I was dragging.

'Yes,' I said. 'What do you think of my chances?'

'What do you call it?'

'*Boogie Nights*.'

'Not a bad concept but it's, you know, a little retro.'

'What are you entering?'

'I'll give you a clue: it happens every twenty-eight days or so.'

'This too will pass,' said Sarah. 'Used or new?'

'Have a look,' said she of the menses. Out of the bag she took a bundle of saturated tampons tied together with a small alarm clock, wires, and batteries, like a time bomb.

'Wow,' I said, 'that's a dynamite entry all right. What's the title?'

'*Annunciation.*'

'Have you ever heard of Cyndie Dubuque?' Sarah asked her.

'No, is she a conceptual artist?'

'Clitoral,' said Sarah. 'Paintings.'

'Sounds very sixties,' said the annunciatory woman, and turned away.

The man behind Sarah was a weedy individual with a quilted anorak, woollen cap, spectacles, pale face, receding chin, burning eyes, and a dustbin. 'What're you entering?' he said, pointing to the parcels on the dolly.

'The dolly,' said Sarah. 'These other things are just stuff I bought on the way here.'

He leered at her in a friendly way. 'Title?'

'*Hello, Dolly.*'

'Not bad, but I think the judges are going to want something a little more serious.'

'Like your dustbin?'

'Right. You can see that it's had a lot of use; it's all dented and battered.' He lifted the lid. 'It's never been washed – smell it. It's empty.'

'No, thank you,' said Sarah. 'What do you call it?'

'The title's down at the bottom, you have to look inside to see it.'

'I won't.'

'All right, you win: it's *My Life*, spelled out in orange peels,' said Weedy, hanging his head modestly.

'You've spelled out your whole life in orange peels?'

'No, no, that's just the title: *My Life*.'

'Poor you!' said Sarah. 'Your life at the bottom of a dustbin. Do you spend much time in it?'

Weedy straightened up sharpish. 'What do you mean?'

'Well, if your life is inside the dustbin, why are you out of it?' said Sarah.

'Are you taking the piss?'

'Never,' said Sarah.

Weedy's eyes started out of his head a little. 'But this isn't to be taken literally,' he sputtered. 'It's a metaphor!'

'For what?'

'My life!'

'Which is what, an empty dustbin?'

'It's empty because it's been purged; all that's left is the orange peel of me!' said Weedy with a vein throbbing in his forehead.

'Then presumably you've eaten the orange?'

'I *was* the orange. It isn't easy talking Art with you.'

'Show me some Art and we'll talk it,' said Sarah.

At that point Weedy gave up on her and started a conversation with a buxom blonde woman behind him who was entering a canvas covered with a brown-paper flap. Weedy showed her his and she showed him hers and although it was a picture of three kittens he seemed to find that he could talk Art with her.

The snow began to fall, the queue inched forward as slowly as ever, and there were no public toilets in sight. Some of those in the queue got others to hold their places while they went into the museum; others who were entering buckets and dustbins may possibly have augmented their entries while screened by sympathetic conceptual artists. Sarah and I took it in turns to visit the museum conveniences and were impressed by them and the exhibition space; the snow sky now had a bright overcast and the variously angled skylights provided a coolly critical daylight that intensified the reality of the entries so far booked in.

There were two men in front of a reception desk and a woman behind it. The men, both heavyset with expressionless faces, looked like builders or movers; the woman might have been cast as a seaside landlady in a black-and-white film. Entrants handed their entrance cards to the woman and were logged in by her. The stamped bottom half of the card was then attached to the entry by the artist. The two men helped unwrap the wrapped entries and waved people on to park their works where they could.

There were many dustbins variously presented along with other concepts and found objects and there were also paintings done by hand and sculptures of recognisable human and animal figures that had the unconfident air of tourists who'd wandered into a rough neighbourhood. Quite possibly there were great works among the entries; I couldn't take in much in a passing glance. I imagined *The One for the Many* among them and I was filled with doubt and confusion. I thought of the eight listening figures in the Orpheus fountain at Cranbrook and shook my head. Sarah had accepted the fact that I myself didn't know what this crucifixion meant and that didn't seem to bother her. She'd confessed that she was a man-improver and I wondered if she saw this work and the entering of it in the competition as an improvement.

The snow stopped, the sun appeared and shed a thin watery

light on the wet winter pavement and our queue as we moved slowly forward along the railings, many of the entrants talking into their little telephones. Behind the three-kitten woman was another woman, young, tall, haggard, scraggy, with what looked like a bag of laundry. She was on the phone rather loudly. 'Of course I did,' she declaimed, 'and I brought your black ones too. No, I didn't; the smell is half the story. Yes, Marcia, it *is* a new idea, because every pile of dirty knickers is different, that's what conceptual is all about: there *are* no two things the same.'

'There,' said Sarah. 'Now we know what conceptual art is all about.'

'What worries me,' I said, 'is, can you catch it from a toilet seat?'

'Easily. Also from oral zeitgeist. Best thing is not to swallow and never sit all the way down.'

'Maybe it's already too late; maybe I'm already conceptual.'

'There's a simple test: if you see vomit on the pavement and don't give it a title you're still OK.'

'Right. I'll keep my eyes open this Saturday night.'

'And now that we've used the c-word,' said Sarah, 'I'm going to come right out and ask you if this might be a concept that we're entering?'

'The one thing I'm sure of is that concepts are not what I'm about.'

'Can you say what you *are* about? I'm just asking – I don't know that I could answer that question myself.'

I pondered that question for a long time. I was thinking about the bonking toys I'd made for Adelbert Delarue; I'd never told Sarah about those. I saw them now in action in all their possible permutations. Those four miniature crash-dummy orgiasts had got me into wood and made me begin to feel like an artist. Feeling that way, I did what artists do: I put an idea into visible form; I couldn't say what the idea was but maybe it would come to me in the fullness of time.

What about religion? To me Christ was not divine, only a charismatic man who died in a horrible way. And as far as I could see, Christianity had done more harm than good in the world. And yet, the idea of a man crowned with thorns dying on a cross – was that something to be taken liberties with? The crucified Christ at St John's in the North End Road was shiny fibreglass but it had no pretensions. Could I say the same for mine? I put my hand in my pocket and felt the small wooden hand Sarah had given me. This whole project had gone from me and I was tired. The salt of it had lost its savour and I wanted to go home.

'UFO Number One, come in, please,' said Sarah.

'Yes,' I said. 'Where were we?'

'Just before you disappeared I asked you what you were about.'

'I can answer that one now, Sarah. I'm about to get all this lumber out of here and go home.'

'How come?'

'Because this thing has gone from me and now it's time for the next thing.'

'What will that be?'

'I don't know yet.'

'Maybe the next thing is to finish this thing.'

'Oh God, you're going to improve me.'

'I warned you.'

'Go ahead, improve.'

'Maybe entering this competition was a bad idea but

walking away from it now would be a failure and I need you not to fail.'

'Why do you see it as a failure?'

'Because whatever this is, you have to get all the way into it before you can get out of it.'

I remembered boyhood fights, not those that I won but the others. When Joe Milanic dared me to knock the chip off his shoulder I did and he made short work of me but at least I hadn't walked away. What about now? From what shoulder had I knocked the chip when I took adze and mallet to the limewood? Well, I'd probably find out if I stayed with it and I'd probably lose Sarah's respect if I didn't. Maybe lose her altogether.

'OK,' I said, 'you've convinced me.'

She looked at me as if my head were transparent and every one of my thoughts was visible to her, especially the last one. 'I think you convinced yourself,' she said, and kissed me.

Now that I had shown Sarah who was in charge I felt a lot better and I also felt like a canoeist being swept towards the edge of Niagara Falls. In no time at all I was over the edge, plunged blindly through the thundering waters, and rose to the surface in front of the builders and movers and the seaside landlady as *Annunciation* was checked in by Ms Menses whose name was actually Philippa Crutchley-Sweet. '*Annunciation*, number seven six o,' said the landlady.

It was very warm in the museum, and the bulkier of the two men had by now rolled up his sleeves to reveal a Sacred Heart tattoo on his left arm and a harp on his right. 'Are you a builder or a concept?' he said as I approached with my timbers.

'You tell me,' I said, indicating the parcels on Sarah's dolly.

'On a building site a two by four is a two by four but here you never know,' he said. 'Let's be having these wrappings off.'

I took a deep breath, undid the twine, and removed the paper from the first parcel. 'Jesus!' he exclaimed as the head and torso came into view.

'*The One for the Many*,' I said.

'Lucky for you we Christians don't do fatwas,' he growled as he flexed his Sacred Heart. 'You can't leave this here in pieces. Put it together and park it somewhere.'

'"But whereunto shall I liken this generation?"' said his colleague. 'Matthew 11.16.'

'*The One for the Many*, your number is seven six one,' said the woman behind the desk with a barely perceptible shake of her head as she stamped my card and handed me the stub.

'You've got to hand in your entry card for that,' said the Hibernian one as he pointed to Sarah's dolly.

'I've changed my mind,' she said. 'I've decided not to enter it after all.'

'"The kingdom of heaven is like unto leaven, which a woman took, and hid in three measures of meal, till the whole was leavened," said he of the gospel. 'Keep it moving, luv. Matthew 13.33.'

Sarah and I restacked the parts of my crucifixion on the dolly; then she pushed it and I carried my cross and other lumber through the already-entered entries until we found enough space to put everything together. I set up the easel to support the figure on its cross. Then I quickly assembled the figure, pegged it to the cross, and pegged the cross to the easel.

There it was then, reared up for the world to see, and I could feel people staring at it – it was impossible *not* to stare. The enormity of what I had done hit me like a ton of bricks, and I half expected my crash-test-dummy-saviour to yell, 'Get me out of here!' but it said nothing. 'Well,' I said to Sarah, 'are you happy now?'

'Are you?'

'I don't know what I am: crazed, I think.'

'Crazed is better than chicken.'

'It's like that, is it?'

'It's all kinds of things, and that's one of them.'

'Righty-o. Well, we've done this. They don't seem to be handing out T-shirts, so we might as well go home now.'

'You're pissed off with me, aren't you?'

'I'm pissed off with myself.'

'Why?'

'I don't know, really. I'm a little short of answers today.'

'So it seems.'

At that moment I was reflecting on how strangers become intimate but at any moment intimates can become strangers again. I'd wrapped the dolly in our discarded brown paper so we could get into a taxi with it, and we walked down to Old Street and found one fairly soon. There we were then, just the two of us in a private space that seemed to be closing in on us.

'It's been a long day,' said Sarah.

'And a hard one. It was one thing to see that piece in my studio, but seeing it in that museum really spooked me.'

'And now you wish you hadn't entered it?'

'I agree with what you said about not walking away from it but I haven't yet been able to get comfortable with the whole thing.'

'Comfort isn't always possible.'

'Maybe I should've had that tattooed on my shoulder instead of a bat.'

'Maybe you should have.' Her voice had an edge to it. We both sank into our thoughts then, and by the time I looked out into the world again we'd come through the City and were on the Embankment. As Westminster Bridge and Boadicea approached we looked up together and looked away again. The Houses of Parliament came and went, the bridges one after the other, the Battersea Power Station with its legs in the air as always. When we were nearing Fulham Sarah said, 'I think you could use an evening to yourself. Could you drop me at my place, please?'

'Certainly.' There was a long silence from there to Doria Road. When we got there I said, 'Can I phone you tomorrow?'

'Please do,' she said. We kissed in a small way and she went into her house. So ended the day in which we entered *The One for the Many* in the R. Albert Streeter Competition.

28

SARAH VARLEY

I didn't realise how lonely I'd been until I stopped being lonely. Not being lonely feels good, as if I'm augmented, more substantial, casting a longer shadow. It also means that I have another person to think of. How's he feeling today, the day after the R. Albert Streeter Museum? What's he thinking, about me in particular? Was I wrong in urging him to enter that competition? How much do I care if I *was* wrong? A lot. This is someone I want to stay with then, is it? Yes. Why do I go for men who, in my opinion, need work? Because they seem capable of change, of becoming, with me, someone they haven't been before. But love changes everyone, doesn't it? Even those who don't need work? Yes, but a man like Roswell has a kind of charm that comes from not being altogether sure of himself and not taking me for granted. When we made love the other night I could feel his happiness and I loved him for it.

How many men have there been between Giles and Roswell? Three that lasted a month or so; two one-nighters. And this . . . ? Looks pretty good to me, OK? OK.

I wish I knew more about him though. We've exchanged histories in a rudimentary way but I've no idea where he is in himself at the moment. There's something bothering him, I know that much.

29

R. ALBERT STREETER

I have left the selection of the judges to Folsom Bray and he has chosen Thurston Fort of the Royal Academy, George Rubcek the art collector, Harvey Stern the sculptor, and Georgiana Crupper the painter. No critics were included and this surprised me. Bray tells me that Fort is open to everything. Rubcek I know about: he has acquired many pieces of rubbish which are now overvalued by many millions. Harvey Stern's sculptures are mostly done by quarry crews who from stone shape huge blocks in which he drills little holes. Georgiana Crupper does horse portraits. Well, Bray is the chair. As Director of the Post-Modern Gallery he was a figure of controversy, and so adroit was he at justifying his actions that it was said of him that he could easily move into politics. The sooner the better, said some. Here I have limited my contribution to money; my opinions I contain in myself.

Fifty works will be accepted for the exhibition. From these will be made a shortlist of ten, one of which will be the winner. The competition is already much talked of and I expect good coverage from the press when the exhibition opens, when the shortlist appears, and when the winner is announced.

From Roswell Clark I have heard nothing since my letter of encouragement in which I wondered what his talent dreams of. *Does* it dream of something more than crash-dummies?

30

ROSWELL CLARK

With the entering of the competition one day behind me I felt much better. Sarah made dinner for us at her place and we became comfortable again. The house was full of bright colours, the bookshelves were well stocked, and there was a print of Caspar David Friedrichs's *Chalk Cliffs on Rugen* with the sheer drop of its white cliffs to the blue sea. In the foreground, seen from behind, are a woman in a red dress pointing down and a man on his hands and knees looking over the edge.

'He's afraid of heights, afraid of falling,' I said, 'and she's pointing down into the drop. What does she want him to do?'

'She's pointing at those little red flowers just on the edge,' said Sarah.

'Ah, yes,' I said, 'and he'll get some for her, too, if the edge doesn't give way.'

'That's what I call a real gentleman,' she said, and we had a quick cuddle. We were in the kitchen, drinking a Minervois, while good smells came from the oven where the lamb was cooking. Boxes and bags of her merchandise stood on the floor, some ready to move out, others in reserve. There was an Egberto Gismonti guitar track going, a warm sound for a winter evening.

'What do you think of this?' said Sarah, holding up a tall narrow vase, in section an ellipse with squared-off ends. It was white porcelain with three Prussian-blue splotches descending from small to large down the front and back.

'It's quite nice; I like it.'

'Sixties, Furstenberg. I paid fifteen for it, might get forty from someone who goes for this kind of thing.'

'I guess it's a matter of finding a punter whose taste is the same as yours.'

'Not always; sometimes I buy things that don't appeal to me but might to somebody else.'

We were sitting in kitchen chairs. She moved hers closer to me and rubbed her shoulder against mine. 'Hi,' I said, and kissed her.

'Hi. How are you feeling about the competition today?'

'As you said, it made sense to finish this thing before going on to the next thing. I have no expectations one way or the other.'

'Any idea what the next thing will be?'

'No. I'm at kind of a funny place in my life.'

'That makes two of us.'

'You're at a funny place in your life?'

'It's the same one where you are. I think we're in it together, yes?'

'Yes. I feel better already.' We hugged and kissed and drank more Minervois. By now the potatoes and beans were boiling, the lamb was almost ready, and the kitchen windows were all steamed up.

'Now that we're both in the same funny place,' said Sarah, 'what can you tell me about *The One for the Many*? I know you said that you don't understand it but you must have some idea where it's coming from.'

'I've told you about my wife's death and my father's and how he became a crash-dummy. I've told you about my Crash Test toy. I haven't told you about my private commissions, which were also of a crash-dummy nature.' I seemed to have too much breath in me so I let some out, then I felt breathless so I breathed in deeply.

'Are you all right?' said Sarah.

'Yes, whew. Actually I've never described them to anyone except the technician who did the motors and connections and the remote control.'

'Take your time. Sounds fascinating.'

'Now I wonder what you'll think of me when I tell you about them.'

'We'll never know unless you do it.'

'True. Well, these were toys of a special kind. First there were the two human figures, male and female crash-dummies, thirty centimetres high, articulated and anatomically complete.'

'You mean, with genitalia?'

'Yes. Working genitalia, and when you pressed a button, they had sexual intercourse. There was a car-crash soundtrack to go with it.'

'Did they have working mouths too?'

'No, just the regular blank dummy faces.'

'So they couldn't even kiss properly.'

'I think that would have compromised their dummyhood. In any case, Delarue didn't ask for working mouths and I didn't suggest them.'

'Delarue is the man who commissioned these figures?'

'Yes, Adelbert Delarue. He lives in Paris.'

'You said those two came first. What came next?'

'A crash-dummy mastiff to the same scale and then a crash-dummy gorilla.'

'Both with working genitalia?'

'Yes.'

'Soundtracks?'

'From *Traviata* with the dog: Callas and "*E strano!*"; Bach's *Passacaglia and Fugue in C Minor* with the gorilla, Schweitzer on the organ.'

'Delarue specified those?'

'No, the soundtracks were my idea but he was delighted with them.'

'And the four dummies going at it in all possible permutations.'

'I suppose so; he liked everything I did.'

'What did he pay you for these figures? Forgive my asking but we market traders always ask these things.'

'Seventy thousand pounds altogether.'

'Crikey! That man must have money to throw around. How did he come to commission you?'

'He got in touch with me after buying the Crash Test toy.'

'What sort of man is he?'

'All I know is that he lives in the Avenue Montaigne, has a girlfriend named Victoria Fawles and a very large chauffeur called Jean-Louis Galantière.'

'How old is he?'

'He hasn't said, but I have a feeling he's a little older than I am, maybe between fifty and sixty.'

'Men!' said Sarah, shaking her head. 'There's another bottle on top of the fridge.' I opened the bottle, refilled our empty glasses, and we clinked. 'Well,' she said, with a smile that hinted at corruptibility, 'this reveals a whole new side of you, not to mention a front and back. Should I be prepared for special requests as we get to know each other better?'

'I'm not the kinky one, Sarah. Delarue told me what he wanted and I did it for the money.'

'What came after the gorilla?'

'I've had no more commissions but he wrote me a letter in which he hoped that his money would buy me time and he wondered what new themes my talent was dreaming of. Not that he wanted to put any pressure on me but of course he did, and so did you.'

'How did I put pressure on you?'

'You know — with your gnostics and your wooden hand and generally wanting me to be better than I am.' I heard myself sounding like a petulant child.

She leaned against me and her lips brushed my face. 'I'm sorry, Roswell,' she murmured, 'I really am. I'll try to do better, I'll work on improving myself.' I couldn't see if her tongue was in her cheek.

'No need to go overboard with it,' I said.

'All right then, let's get back to the matter at hand: what was there between the bonking toys and the crucifixion?'

'Nothing special.' As I said that, St John's in the North End Road, Abraham Selby and the fibreglass Jesus came to me with the freshness of rain and the earth smell of yellow leaves. 'I fainted,' I said. 'His eyes went blank in the rain.'

'Whose eyes?'

'The fibreglass Jesus at St John's in the North End Road.'

'His eyes went blank and you fainted?'

'I'd been drinking that morning. Father John got me out of the rain and into the church.'

'Are you religious, Roswell?'

'No.'

'But you were what – standing in the rain looking at Jesus on his cross?'

'He was in the rain too; I don't know why they bother with that little tiny roof over the INRI.'

'Do you often stop to look at him?'

'Now and then. Sometimes I get into a conversation with one of the guys from the low-budget drinking community.'

'And it was after the fainting that you started your crucifixion?'

'Yes.'

'How soon?'

'I ordered the wood the next day, started work on the figure two days after that. The adze bit me the first time I hit it with the mallet. That's all I know about where that crucifixion's coming from. Does that make it all clear to you?'

'No. You're a man of mystery.'

'How about that. Did you ever think you'd meet one?'

'Not really, but I kept hoping. Some day my prince will come, I thought.'

'Well, here I am: you wished long enough and strong enough and wishing made it so.'

No answer. She was asleep with her head on my shoulder and the second bottle was empty.

31

SARAH VARLEY

One day followed another while the judges deliberated. Roswell and I spent every night together, sometimes at my place, sometimes at his; falling asleep together made the world look a lot better when we woke up. Mostly I cooked for us but at the end of our first week Roswell took me to The Blue Elephant in Fulham Broadway: we sat among the plants in the moist and jungly air and listened to the splashing of water while we drank house white and ate little golden parcels of spicy Thai esoterica followed by more advanced esoterica with unknown vegetables.

I'm surprised at how often drink occurs in my narration. One Monday evening after my return from Covent Garden I was unwinding with my feet on the table and a glass of Australian Chardonnay in my hand when Roswell turned up. 'You're looking at a rejectee,' he said, and showed me a card from the R. Albert Streeter Museum. It said simply that his entry had not been accepted for the exhibition and gave the hours when it could be collected.

'I suppose I'm out of touch with the art world,' I said. 'I was sure it would be accepted.'

'I'm glad it wasn't,' he said. 'I've done my part – that thing's finished now and I can move on to the next thing.'

'Which is?'

'I don't know yet: whatever it happens to be.'

He certainly seemed happier than he'd been when we entered the piece in the competition. We went to his place after we'd eaten; he took me up to the studio, produced a large cartridge-paper drawing pad and a stick of conté sanguine, and asked me to disrobe.

'What have you got in mind?' I said.

'Short poses,' said Roswell. 'You can undress behind the screen and there's a clean robe for you to put on in the rest periods.'

'Very professional!'

'I have to keep my mind on my work.'

'Sketches for a Boadicea, are these?'

'Don't make fun of yourself – you're not a small woman, but you're a beauty.'

'I don't think I've been called that before.'

'Get used to it. Having seen you naked, I want to draw you, just for the pleasure of doing it.'

'I can deny you nothing,' I said, and retired behind the screen to get naked. When I reappeared I saw that Roswell had moved a Lloyd Loom chair to the centre of the room and placed a couple of pillows on it. The drawing pad was on an easel facing it. He arranged me on the chair, humming a little to himself, then stepped back and looked at me purposefully. I felt my nipples stiffen and reminded myself to think pure thoughts. My left arm was at an angle that allowed me to see the bat tattoo on my shoulder and I smiled, fancying that Roswell's bat was talking to mine.

The conté crayon rasped on the paper as his hand moved

quickly. He finished the sketch, tore it off the pad, laid it on the floor, and began another. He was looking different from how I'd seen him before – more like a person to be reckoned with. Each pose lasted only five minutes, and after twenty minutes Roswell called a rest period. I modestly put on my robe and went to look at the sketches that were lying on the floor. I was surprised at how good they were, how authoritative: with a few strokes he'd caught the gesture of each pose and the gesture contained the whole body. 'I didn't know you could draw like this,' I said.

'I didn't either,' he said. 'Best not to talk about it or it might go away.'

The next poses were standing, then he put a blanket and cushions on the floor and drew me lying down or half reclining. Altogether we worked for about an hour with a rest after the second twenty minutes. At the end of the hour he said, 'Thank you, Sarah,' and hugged me and kissed me. All of the sketches were good; they were fierce with life, and I marvelled at their having come from looking at me.

The next day Roswell phoned Nigel and that afternoon we went to Hoxton to collect *The One for the Many*. Traffic around the museum was heavy but not gridlocked. Rejected entries and their owners cluttered the pavement waiting to be picked up while newer rejectees swarmed into the museum. Nigel dropped us off and we went inside with our dolly, brown paper, and twine. The rejected entries were ticketed with red cards. 'Nice touch, that,' said Roswell.

When we found the crash-dummy crucifixion there was a small crowd around it that included the Hibernian man and the scripture-quoting one from our first visit. There was a babble of voices from those gathered around *The One for the Many*. 'I saw it,' said someone. 'I saw a tear rolling down his face.'

'From what?' said a sceptic. 'He's got no eyes to cry with.'

'Let's not be blocking traffic here,' said the Hibernian. 'Them tears is condensation from the skylight – you get that with changes of temperature.'

'O ye of little faith!' said the scriptural one. 'I've already moved it to a different position and a new tear rolled down his face.'

'Don't be stupid,' said the Hibernian. 'Jesus wouldn't waste a tear on this lot. Let's keep moving, folks – people are here to collect their entries.'

'Excuse us, please,' said Roswell, elbowing his way through. 'This one's mine.'

'He's not just yours,' said a woman with bulging eyes. 'He's the one for the many, he crashed for our sins.'

'Do me a favour,' said Roswell, as a nearby camera flashed.

'Move it again,' said a man, 'and let's see if there's a new tear.' He grabbed Roswell's arm.

'You want something to cry about?' said Roswell.

'None of that here,' said the Hibernian. 'Take it outside.' He cleared a space for Roswell who took the figure from the cross and dismantled it.

'God sees what you do,' said the bulging-eyed woman.

'Right,' said Roswell. 'He's got his eye on you too.' We loaded the disassembled figure on the dolly and covered it with brown paper. Then Roswell gathered up the timbers of the cross and the easel and we made our way to the exit. Nigel and the van appeared shortly and we loaded up and headed for Kempson Road. Roswell and I sat there shaking our heads over the scene in the museum.

'Jesus wept,' I said.

'Them tears was condensation,' said Roswell. 'Although that competition was enough to make a dummy weep. I'm glad it's behind us.'

'Me too,' I said, and squeezed his hand.

We found a parking space in Kempson Road and Roswell shouldered his cross (in pieces) and the easel up to the studio while I followed with the head and torso of *The One for the Many* and Nigel was behind me with the limbs and dolly. Roswell paid Nigel and there we were then, purged?

'What now?' I said.

'It's almost drinks time but not quite,' said Roswell. If I'd just met him at that moment I'd never have thought of him as a failed person. He removed the chromium crown of thorns from the head, put it in a vice, and crushed it, then he clamped the torso in a larger wooden bench vice, plugged in a power saw, and started cutting. The action and whine of the saw and the smell of the sawdust made it very much a man thing, and I could see that he was feeling good about it. I was feeling good too. When Roswell finished with the torso and head he cut up the limbs, then the cross. It took rather a long time but I sat there patiently, dying for a drink.

When *The One for the Many* was reduced to firewood Roswell fetched the firewood basket from the living room and loaded it up, then we carried it down between us. It was the right evening for a fire and the wood burned fiercely with blue flames and the sweetish smell of the glue and varnish. 'OK, guv, what are we drinking?' I said as I settled myself on the couch.

'Champagne to start with,' said Roswell. 'There may be some in the fridge.'

'What're we celebrating?'

'Feeling good. Is that reason enough?'

'Always.' Just then the doorbell rang.

'I'm not expecting anyone,' said Roswell, and went to answer it. I heard voices and after a while he came back, shaking his head. 'That was a reporter from the *Evening Standard*,' he said. 'He was at the museum this afternoon and wanted to talk to me about the weeping Jesus. I told him it was condensation and then he wanted a closer look at the piece. I told him that wasn't possible and got rid of him.'

'That weeping was strange, though, wasn't it?'

'Yes, it was. I'm glad we got that dummy out of there before the hysteria really took hold.'

'But you must have been a little bit spooked – I know I was.'

'Sure I was. For a moment I thought it was weeping because it didn't want to die for my sins. That's how weird I am.'

I started to say something but then I thought it better to leave him to his thoughts. And me to mine.

He went down to the kitchen and came back with two flutes and the champagne in a plastic cooling bucket. He pulled the cork and filled our glasses with the bright foaming Moët & Chandon. 'Here's to you, Sarah,' he said as we clinked. 'You really have improved me.'

'Here's looking at you, Roswell, you've improved both of us.' So we didn't need to say anything more for quite a long time as we drank and leaned against each other and looked at the fire, while outside the winter evening breathed its cold breath on the windows and passersby in the darkness looked up at our golden oblongs of cosiness. It's always surprising how things that are very complex and improbable become by degrees quite simple and as if they're the only possible outcome of everything that has gone before. It was good not having to lean forward any more to help Roswell push his stone uphill.

The next day on a sudden impulse I bought a *Standard* and turned, as if with prescience, to the page with the cartoon and the various snippets. There it was: a photograph of Roswell and the hyperthyroid woman in front of *The One for the Many*. The story followed:

JESUS WEPT?

Ms Ernestine Casey and Mr Roswell Clark discuss *The One for the Many*, Mr Clark's rejected entry in the R. Albert Streeter competition. Ms Casey and several others claim to have seen tears rolling down the face of the crucified crash-test dummy. The museum staff say that this was caused by condensation from the skylight. Mr Clark had nothing to add to this when interviewed at his home, and said that the figure was not available for inspection.

'Aha!' I said to myself. 'I bet Roswell gets one or two phone calls before the day is over.'

When he came to my place that evening we both showed our *Standards* and said, 'Have you seen this?' Then we both laughed and said yes, we had. 'I had a phone call as well,' he said. 'Guess who from?'

'George Rubcek?'

'How'd you know?'

'First name that came into my head. What'd he say?'

'He said he was sorry my piece hadn't been accepted for the exhibition but he'd been outvoted. Then he offered me seventy-five thousand pounds for it. When I told him I'd burnt it he laughed and said that was one way of making a creative experience complete and he hoped I'd stay in touch.'

'Seventy-five thousand pounds! It takes me six years to make that much! Are you sorry you burnt it?'

'No. It's not as if the burning of it cost me that amount of money – I did what I needed to do to get from one thing to the next; I wasn't manufacturing something for sale, and the value put on it by a would-be purchaser is irrelevant.'

'My hero,' I said.

There were no other journalistic enquiries about the weeping Jesus and nothing further in the press that we heard of. In due course the R. Albert Streeter prize was announced. It was won by one of the dustbin entries, not Weedy's orange-peel effort but one that featured eggshells and coffee grounds. A young woman called Prismatica Froude was the proprietor of this dustbin. Folsom Bray, as director of the museum and chairman of the judges, issued this statement:

We live in a time of constant change and constantly changing perceptions. Governments are having to recognise that their world-views are not always shared by those they govern, and cultural establishments find themselves in the same situation. In art as in world affairs there are groundswells that compel us to reassess what we have always taken for granted and to redefine art itself.

In the primeval caves of France and Spain, among the astonishing drawings of animals, there can be seen negative handprints made by placing the hand with outspread fingers against the cave wall and blowing powdered red ochre or blue-black manganese around it and between the fingers. Startling in its immediacy, this ancient image says, 'Look! With this hand I take hold of the world.'

Through the centuries the world has seen what the hands of Leonardo, Michelangelo, Rembrandt, Vermeer, and other masters have achieved. Can the hand and the mind be separated? Or is the mind really the primal and the primary hand? Henri Focillon, in his classic meditation, *The Life of Forms in Art*, cites Hokusai's demonstration in which he placed a scroll of blank paper on the floor, poured a pot of blue paint over it, then dipped the claws of a rooster in a pot of red paint and let the bird run across the paper. Those viewing the result found in it the image of a familiar stream carrying the red maple leaves of autumn. The mind of Hokusai used for its hand the feet of a rooster; and the minds of the viewers became the hand that drew a recognisable image.

There were fourteen hundred and twenty-three entries in this competition and they separated themselves into various categories of works that could be grouped together. Dustbins, tampons, and underwear were three of these categories, dustbins being the most numerous: there were ninety-seven of them, empty or full in their different ways but unanimous in their perception of the human condition in the world of today. There are no two dustbins the same but they speak with one voice, the voice of the mind that is the supreme hand. In the eggshells and coffee grounds of the winning entry, in these entrails of our nights and mornings each of us may descry a different future but whatever comes, we must work through it together, no two of us the same.

'There you have it,' I said. 'Nobody can bray like Folsom.'

'He's the man, all right,' said Roswell. 'I need you to take your clothes off again.'

'Are you going to take advantage of me, squire?'

'First a few longer poses,' he said, and followed me up to the studio. When I was *au naturel* he had no chair for me, only the blanket on the floor. 'What I want,' he said, 'is you in various attitudes of listening: standing, sitting, lying down – as many different ones as you can think of.'

'Listening?'

'Listening.'

'For what?'

'That we don't know yet,' he said. 'It could take years.'

So there I was, wearing nothing but my bat tattoo. Which seemed to have a lot of lift in it. 'Yes,' I said, 'I believe it could.'

32

R. ALBERT STREETER

To be a patron of the arts of painting and sculpture has been my delight. But now do I question whether I had not done better to buy a soccer team or found a leper colony. The competition to which I gave my name at the museum of the same name has produced a catalogue of fifty entries. I ask myself for what have these been chosen, what attributes? There is of course a place for dustbins and their contents, for used tampons and dirty underwear, but I weep to think that my museum is that place. Is this all there is?

'Be tranquil,' I say to myself. 'It does not import, no.' The money comes in faster than I can spend it. In my pocket it lights a fire and I extinguish this fire in one way or another. Sometimes with a Peng, sometimes with a whimper.

Ennui is the enemy constantly to be fought; cries once passionate become, with time, yawns of boredom. Someone has sent me a cutting from a London newspaper in which appears a photograph of Roswell Clark with a crash-dummy crucifixion. To this I say both 'Ho-hum' and 'Thank you, no'. A crucified crash-dummy is not, may I say, *comme il faut*? 'Anything goes,' says an old song. But although one may take the boy out of the Jesuits one does not take the Jesuits out of the boy. Indeed, I have had enough of crash-dummies; they are so 'last-year', as one says. I had high hopes for Clark, and perhaps he may yet do something from which will spread ever-widening ripples; I wish him luck but my interest has moved elsewhere.

As to automata, couplings whether human or bestial, however diverse the partners, are of limited stimulation; horror has more depth in its eroticism. On my table the dark wood surrounds the little man; whichever way he turns, the horrible hopping thing is behind him; always it overtakes him as he knows it will. Does he perhaps long for this consummation? Does his desire incline to this ultimate surrender?

M. R. James is indeed *premier cru* but in H. P. Lovecraft might there be a riper, non-Euclidean delight – a more delicious shudder? Yes, I wonder what Dieter Scharf will do with Cthulhu, rising from the deeps of the ancient past to find love. Doing it his way.

A NOTE ON THE AUTHOR

Russell Hoban is the author of many extraordinary novels including *Turtle Diary*, *Riddley Walker*, *Angelica's Grotto*, and most recently *The Bat Tattoo*. He has also written some classic books for children including *The Mouse and His Child* and the Frances books. He lives in London.

His new novel, *Her Name Was Lola*, will be published by Bloomsbury in 2003.

RIDDLEY WALKER Russell Hoban £6.99 0 7475 5904 X

A Twentieth-Anniversary Edition with an Introduction by Will Self

Walker is my name and I am the same. Riddley Walker. Walking my riddels where ever theyve took me and walking them now on this paper the same.

Composed in an English which has never been spoken and laced with a storytelling tradition that predates the written word, *Riddley Walker* is the world waiting for us at the bitter end of the nuclear road. Desolate, dangerous and harrowing, it is a modern masterpiece.

'This is what literature is meant to be' Anthony Burgess

AMARYLLIS NIGHT AND DAY Russell Hoban £6.99 0 7475 5381 5

The first time Peter Diggs saw Amaryllis was in a dream. She was at a bus stop where the street sign said Balsamic, although there was nothing vinegary about the place. The bus was unthinkably tall, made of yellow, orange and pink rice paper, lit from within like a Japanese lantern. 'Trust me, I'm a weirdo,' says Amaryllis as she and Peter embark on their nocturnal experimentation, which leaves no one on quite the same footing with reality…

'Tantalising, fresh and inventive … Hoban writes about grown-up love with an extraordinary unsentimental yearning' *Literary Review*

THE MEDUSA FREQUENCY Russell Hoban £6.99 0 7475 5909 0

An inexplicable message flashing on the screen of his computer at 3 a.m. heralds the beginning of a startling quest for frustrated author Herman Orff. Taking up the offer of a cure for writer's block leads him 'to those places in your head that you can't get to on your own', and plunges him into a world inhabited by a combination of characters from myth and reality: the talking head of Orpheus; a lost love; the young girl of Vermeer's famous portrait — and a frequency of Medusas.

'Russell Hoban is our Ur-novelist, a maverick voice that is like no other' *Sunday Telegraph*

To order from Bookpost PO Box 29 Douglas Isle of Man IM99 1BQ www.bookpost.co.uk email: bookshop@enterprise.net fax: 01624 837033 tel: 01624 836000

bloomsburypbks

www.bloomsbury.com/russellhoban

Are you interested in literature?

From John Irving to Lesley Glaister, David Guterson to Donna Tartt, and from first-time authors to Booker Prize winners, Bloomsbury Publishing brings you an exciting new opportunity to explore the world of literature with the launch of the **Bloomsbury Reading Club**.

Whether you are in a book group or just an interested reader, the Bloomsbury Reading Club will have something for you.

As a member of the Bloomsbury Reading Club you will have access to some of the world's greatest authors and an inside track on the latest literary events. Simply sign up today – free! – and enjoy a range of benefits including:

A bi-monthly newsletter
Competitions
Reading Club discounts on selected books
Pre-publication previews of hot new titles
Early booking and ticket concessions for big events
The chance to ask authors about their writing
Recommendations from Bloomsbury editors

Why not join up today?

You can join for free at www.bloomsbury.com/readersgroups